BY NOW, NOVARO had calmed enough to really study how MacGregor handled his boat. Once they'd entered the open sea, Mac had been forced to be very deliberate about his movements - not only to stay ahead but to weather the heavy waves. Before this moment, Novarro had tried to kill MacGregor, not his boat. Now he realized his error. Focusing on a larger target—especially a moving one—made more sense.

He took slow, determined aim. His sights found the place where he knew the gas tank would be. A wave ran under his boat, and the nose bumped up, throwing off his aim.

"Steady," he hissed at Hanson.

Hanson held it steady.

He found the gas tank again and, without hesitating, trusted his instinct and fired.

Mac's boat became a ghastly ball of flame and black smoke. Novarro gloated at the fiery rain—the fallout from Mac's destroyed boat that drifted down, hissing, into the sea.

"May you burn in Hell, MacGregor," he said.

"Amen to that, brother," Hanson agreed.

ABOUT THE AUTHOR

ALLAN COLE is an international best-selling author, screenwriter and former prize-winning newsman. The son of a CIA operative, Cole was raised in the Middle East, Europe and the Far East. His works include The Timura Trilogy, Lucky In Cyprus, Tales Of The Blue Meanie, My Hollywood MisAdventures, The Shannon Trilogy and The Hate Parallax, which he wrote with Russian fantasy master, Nick Perumov. He's also known as the co-author of the popular Sten Series - which he wrote with the late Chris Bunch. Allan has published more than two dozen books and sold more than 150 screenplays. For further details visit his website at http://www.acole.com. He's also listed at Wikipedia.com and IMBD.com.

MacGregor In: Dying Good

by

Allan Cole

For Kathryn
The love of my life

Copyright 2011 By Allan Cole
ISBN-13: 978-0615522050
ISBN-10 061552205X

CHAPTER ONE

THE OLD DUGOUT crashed out of the reeds, sending half-a-dozen swamp hens racing across the lily pads for cover. One of them was too slow, and when the prow butted into it the bird took flight, bursting up into the girl's face.

As panicked as the bird, the girl swerved, jamming the boat's broad nose into the hairy roots of a mangrove. She lashed frantically with her paddle, trying to get free. She slapped at the water, the reeds—everything and anything to get unstuck from those roots. The boat swayed this way and that, like a trapped manatee trying to escape the sharp blades of a propeller.

Engines suddenly roared somewhere behind her, and Marie, who was no more than thirteen, stifled a cry then dug deep into the water to finally break free. She back-paddled a few strokes then shot forward, her fear-powered arms making the leaky old boat fly across the lake's surface like a water skimmer chased by wide-mouthed bass.

The engine roar grew louder and the girl paddled harder, but this time she didn't panic. Drawing on all her strength, she fought for calm, concentrating on her task. She was a strong little girl—a shrimper's daughter—and her small hands were calloused and sure from four years at her mother's side, fixing nets and cleaning shrimp. She kept the dugout straight and true, even though the paddle's edges were as rough as the old gutting knife her brother put under his bed at night to fend off the tough men who came around to take an honest shrimper's earnings.

The shore was just ahead, beckoning with its muddy banks and thick tropical foliage that could hide a child like Marie from her pursuers.

Then the airboat crashed out of the reed thicket behind her, riding high and fast over the swamp grass that had tangled her paddle. There was a tough young Latina steering the airboat, and when she spotted Marie she shouted at her boyfriend, a scrawny, sunburned Florida cracker:

"There she is, Tampa."

Tampa, whose eyes were much sharper than his wits, swiveled his ropy neck, low forehead furrowed under sweat-streaked hair, until he finally fixed on the dugout and the girl.

"Got 'er, Bonita. Pour it on, honey."

Bonita poured it on, feeding so much Texaco joy juice to those twin Chevy engines that they lifted the airboat right out of the water and sent it surging after the girl.

Marie heard the airboat closing in but didn't waste breath crying out. She put her fear into paddling, aiming for that quickly approaching shore. Behind her, Bonita had the airboat moving so fast and so sure that she jumped the vessel over a grassy hummock as smoothly as a big gator going for its prey. Even so, Marie was strong for her size and determined enough for anybody's size, and she drove that old dugout to shore so hard it jammed into the mud bank.

She didn't hesitate a second, bounding out of the dugout to hit the ground running. First, she sprinted for the brush that lined the trail. But the brambles were too sharp and thick; and she fell back, sobbing, her bare arms cut and bleeding.

Bonita skidded the airboat into the shore, sending up a wave that nearly sank the dugout. Marie whirled and raced down the dirt path that circled the lake, looking for a way through the heavy foliage.

At the airboat, Bonita throttled back the engines and bumped against the bank. Tampa jumped and scrambled onto the path.

"I'll cut her off, hon," Bonita shouted and spun the airboat around to race along the shoreline.

Tampa sprinted after Marie, who was a good fifty yards ahead, his long, skinny legs quickly closing the gap.

Marie heard Tampa's booted feet getting closer, and she dug into the last of her reserve to put on a burst of speed. Gradually, she pulled away. Off to the side, she heard the

Allan Cole

airboat skimming along the bank. But Bonita had to stay with the boat and couldn't get at her.

The girl rushed toward a gnarled log lying across the path. As she started to jump the log suddenly came alive. The front end turned toward her and split in half, exposing enormous rows of white teeth. It was a big gator; and as it turned, it hissed and lashed its tail.

Marie was too scared to scream. She started to back away; then she tripped and, with a small cry, tumbled onto the ground. She heard the hissing gator coming, and then Tampa's long shadow fell across her.

Marie looked up and saw the skinny redneck draw his .45. He took careful aim at the gator and fired... once... twice. And it was over. The reptile grunted and died.

Tampa leaned over and grabbed the girl by the wrist with his free hand.

"Gotcha," he said, laughing.

But Marie fought him, kicking and flailing.

"Now cut that out," Tampa said, shaking her. "Didn't I just save you from that mean ole gator?"

Marie was far from grateful. She sank her sharp teeth into his wrist, and Tampa howled in pain and fury.

"Goddamn, you little skunk ass," he bellowed.

He threw the girl to the ground and raised his pistol.

Behind him, Bonita had beached the airboat and was hurrying over to him. She saw what he was about to do.

"Tampa, don't," she shouted.

He was so furious he paid her no mind. Tampa fired— Boom! Just like that.

Not one second of hesitation.

Bonita ran up. She looked at Marie's body. Then up at her redneck boyfriend. She sighed a sigh of weary resignation, and Tampa was suddenly embarrassed. He hung his head. Just like a little boy, she thought.

"Oh, Tampa, sweetie pie," she said. "What did you do, hon?"

"I couldn't help it, Bonita, baby," Tampa whined. "She went and bit me."

7

Allan Cole

Bonita sighed again. "That just cost us five hundred dollars, baby. Didn't I tell you we needed a new septic tank for the RV park?"

Tampa started to get irritated. "Okay, okay," he said. "Geeze, Louise. I hate it when you bug me about money, hon." He looked down at the girl and shrugged. "Least she won't bite no more."

Allan Cole

CHAPTER TWO

THE JEEP BOOMED down Ocean Boulevard, stereo
blaring a rap song, a topless blonde standing in the seat
twirling her bikini top over her head while she whooped and
hollered and gave all the drivers a micro-bikini eyeful. She
was a South Florida vision to die for. Beside her an earnest
young black kid was thinking more about the death part as he
squirmed in his seat, hands gripping the wheel, scared
spitless and begging the girl to sit the hell down.

"Goddamn, Kim," he moaned. "We're supposed to start
rehab tomorrow morning."

But Kim just kept on shaking her stuff. "Come on, Jean."
she shouted. "Last day to party."

All around her, four lanes of young men leaned out of
their cars to cheer Kim on.

"Go, baby, go. Take it all off." All the while snapping
live cell-phone postcards of the wild life, Boca Raton style,
to beam home to envious friends.

Horns blared, tires squealed; and more than a few
fenders were bent as Kim wriggled to the beat, with only the
padded roll bar keeping her from tumbling out.

A police siren howled into life, and Kim's companion
jolted up to see the red gumball light rotating in his rearview
mirror.

"Oh, man," Jean moaned. "Uncle Mac's gonna shit
nickels."

Then it was instant panic city time as Jean mashed the
accelerator and sped away, Boca Raton's finest in hot pursuit
and Kim doing an amazing balancing act, twirling her bikini
bra and swiveling her hips.

* * *

A mile or so up the coast, tucked between the Red Reef
Golf Course and a million-dollar-a-unit condo complex, was
an old beach house. Three weathered stories staggered up the
high grassy bluff that bordered South Ocean Boulevard and
ran down in a series of dunes to the sea. There were railed
sundecks circling each floor of the house, and a wide
sundeck planked across the roof.

Across the highway and framing the top story of the
house was Spanish River Park, a tropical wonderland of
exotic trees and wildlife that included everything from
gators, to raccoons, to girls like Kim in tiny bikinis. Except
they were soaking up rays for all over tans instead of playing
topless go-go girls in Jeeps.

The face of the house was all windows, set in old-
fashioned frames that gazed out at the warm seas of the
Atlantic. To the left of the stairs were several red-flagged
wire barriers, put there to protect sea turtle nests. The posted
barriers were required by state and Palm Beach County laws.
Few Boca residents objected, just as they didn't object to the
city ordinance requiring all beach dwellers to douse their
outdoor lights at night during the hatching season. The lights,
it seemed, led the baby turtles astray as they swam for the
starry horizons programmed in their genes.

Normally, a sailboard rested in the sand to the right of
the stairs, but on this particular day the yellow-and-black-
striped board with its opaque yellow sail was swooping
gracefully through the surf. It carried a tall, tanned man with
an athletic build, dark hair streaked by the sun and
experience and pale blue eyes set deep under furrowed
brows. He wore faded red boxer trunks and leaned far out
over the water, coaxing his board through the waves.

This was the "Uncle Mac" Jean had predicted would
"shit nickels" when he found out what his wards were up to.
He had a lot more names than Mac. Addison Mizner Flagler
Titus Broward MacGregor could also be listed. There were
others. So many, Mac liked to say, that if they were "laid end
to end we'd have one helluva orgy and mass arrest."

Allan Cole

Mac was related to just about everybody who was anybody of historical interest in the state of Florida—from ex-governors to ex-horse thieves. His mother's maiden name was Mizner—for the Addison Mizner who created Boca Raton out of a swamp and then promoted it shamelessly until it became one of the most exclusive beach communities in the world. Her mother had been a Flagler, after the oil tycoon who had built Florida's first railroad.

Mac's late father, Frank MacGregor, was a descendant of a soldier of fortune who in 1817 briefly replaced the Spanish flag in Florida with his own.

Despite this background, Mac was not a man of wealth or property. Nor did he covet same. Besides the historic names and the old beach house and its contents, about the only thing of value he possessed was the classic, 1987 YJ Wrangler Jeep that, unbeknownst to him, was racing toward the house with the police in hot pursuit.

Mac shifted position on his board and glanced over at the house, wondering how much time he had before lunch. On the lower sundeck he could see the small figure of Stormy, his housekeeper, and the even smaller figure of her granddaughter, Leslie. The two were energetically sweeping the deck, working their way toward the double patio doors that led into his den.

Good. He had time to play a little longer.

Mac came about, let the wind catch the sail, and bounded over a rolling wave.

*   *   *

Stormy reached the den then stashed the broom and got out the vacuum cleaner. Leslie was two months past her tenth birthday - the age at which children are either eager to help or eager to hide from anything involving work. Leslie was of the eager-to-help variety and was careful to find all the various tools to the vacuum.

Stormy unwound the cord and handed the plug to the girl.

"Here, honey bun," she said, "plug it in for your old grandma."

Allan Cole

While Leslie ran to do her bidding, she turned to run a dirt-and-dust-wary eye over Mac's den. Stormy Nichols was a small, skinny woman of indeterminate age. In the steamy Florida heat, she wore cutoffs and a halter top that showed off the scores of fabulous tattoos that decorated her body. She was an ex-biker princess, a woman with a hard mouth for her enemies and a soft heart for those close to her—with a special warmth for Leslie and Mac.

Mac's was a fairly typical male domain--dark wood, old-fashioned desk with a new-fashioned computer—an IMac, naturally. One wall was crammed with books, another slathered with framed photographs—mostly of Mac posing with the famous and the infamous, ranging from politicians and entertainment industry stars to sportsmen and business people. The photos weren't there for mere boasting purposes; they represented how Mac made his living. When potential new clients sought him out, he brought them into the den, where they couldn't help but notice the pictures, then invited them to offer what they chose for payment.

It wasn't necessarily money Mac sought, and he made this known right from the start. When it came to money, Mac was a firm believer in his great-uncle Mizner's adage: "Money, to be worth striving for, must have blood and perspiration on it—preferably that of someone else."

Besides, Mac thought money was weighted down with too many encumbrances. Money required safekeeping, careful thought, and the continuous acquisition of more. It also required documents that had to be submitted to various governmental bodies and institutions, obligations he detested.

An obligation to another person—a human being—was a different matter, however. He not only didn't dislike such obligations, he welcomed them. Paid his mortgage, taxes, upkeep on the Jeep, Stormy's salary and fun and recreation with those obligations.

He called this process "trading favors." Each photograph on the mantle represented somebody Mac had helped get out of a jam, many of which were life-threatening, or career threatening.

Allan Cole

The only photo on display for prideful reasons was one of him astride his favorite polo pony, with a trophy in his lap that he'd won at the Palm Beach Polo Grounds. Grinning up at him was actor Tommy Lee Jones, who ran a string of ponies on the circuit and sometimes asked Mac to fill in if one of his regular riders was injured or sick. The trophy had been won on one of those days.

Mac looked so ridiculously pleased with himself that Stormy had to laugh every time she saw that picture. She flicked the vacuum on and approached the photo, feather duster raised. Stormy paused a moment, studying Mac's exotic features: he was a mixture of so many breeds that he looked unlike anyone she had never known. He had an Irishman's thick, curly hair – naturally dark, but streaked from the sun. His eyes were Irish blue, his high cheekbones American Indian, but his other features were a mixture of Portuguese, a touch of Italian, and a bit of what Mac said was probably African-American.

"Don't know if it's absolutely true, or not," he liked to say. "But if it rattles people's cage when I announce my possible heritage, I know whether I want to be friends or not."

Stormy got a kick out of her boss's handsome looks and how they made women's hearts jump. But she did think that at times - with his gleaming white smile - that he looked too satisfied with himself.

"I'm gonna wipe that grin right off of your mush, Mac," she said, and ran the brush over the picture.

Just then Leslie ran up to her, tugging at her leg.

"Grandma," she cried. "Come look."

She pulled Stormy to the curtained window. Stormy frowned when she saw flashing red lights glaring through the fabric.

"What are they doing, Grandma?" the child cried.

Stormy only grunted. Then she cautiously twitched the curtains aside.

13

Allan Cole

CHAPTER THREE

SHE PEERED THROUGH the gap in the curtain. The window overlooked Mac's driveway, where she could see Jean and a still-topless Kim backed up against the garage wall. Two squad cars blocked the Jeep, and as she watched several cops climbed out, some with their guns drawn.

Immediately, Stormy spun around and ran to Mac's desk. She yanked open a drawer, pulled out a flare gun and ran out onto the sundeck, Leslie at her heels. She spotted Mac on his sailboard skimming just off shore. She raised the flare gun and fired.

*   *   *

Mac was about to turn back out to sea; but just as he leaned to make the maneuver, he saw fingers of red explode out of a fiery ball in the sky. What the hell, he thought, turning to find Stormy and Leslie waving frantically at him from the sundeck.

He didn't waste time wondering what it was about. Stormy was not a person who panicked at life's trifles. If she fired the flare gun, something was definitely up.

Mac shifted his weight, skillfully turned the board, and raced to the shore. He hit the sand, pulled the sailboard up onto the beach, and sprinted to the house. A minute later he bounded up the wooden stairs to the lower deck where Stormy waited, Leslie hiding shyly behind her.

"What's wrong?" he asked.

Stormy shook her head, so agitated her tats looked like they were trying to jump off her skin.

"Pigs," she said, almost spitting the word. "Pigs is what's wrong."

Mac lifted an eyebrow. "What are they doing?"

She shrugged. "Pig shit," she replied, as if—what else?

Leslie was shocked. "Grandma said pig shit, Uncle Mac," she said, running to Mac and throwing her arms around his leg. "Did you hear? She said pig shit clear as day."

Stormy shook her head. "God forgive me," she said, "but I just purely hate cops."

Mac laughed and untangled Leslie from his leg.

"Stormy can't help it, Leslie," he said. "She was raised that way." He nodded at Stormy. "Okay, let's see what these gallant forces of the law are up to."

Mac grabbed an oversized Hawaiian shirt off a beach chair and shrugged it on as he went to the side gate. The shirt hung loosely, emphasizing his lean, muscular structure. He paused to get his act together, then lifted the latch, pushed the gate aside and walked into madness.

Jean and the topless Kim cowered against the garage as several Boca cops, led by a beefy patrolman with a weightlifter's build and steroid temper, advanced on them with their guns drawn. The namctag on the steroid cop's shirt read Officer Maass.

"Thank God, you're home, Uncle Mac," Jean said.

"They're gonna arrest us, Uncle Mac," Kim wailed. "And we didn't do anything. Honest."

Before Maass and the others could stop him, Mac stalked over to the couple. He peeled off his shirt and draped it around Kim. Out of the corner of his eye he noticed a look of disappointment on several cop faces as her pretty breasts and round hips vanished beneath his extra-large Hawaiian shirt.

"That's okay, officers," he told them. "I'll take over from here."

The cops were dumbfounded, especially Maass.

"The hell you will," he snarled. "They're goin' to the station, pal."

Mac gave him a mild look. "That won't be necessary..." He peered at the nametag. "...Officer Maass. Call your lieutenant, she'll set you straight."

"Just who the hell are you?" Maass demanded.

Mac nodded at the kids. "Their cousin."

Maass sneered. "They called you uncle." He gave Jean a pointed look then glared at Mac. "Which is just as big a lie."

Mac sighed wearily. "No lie," he said. "We really are cousins, but they call me uncle. The age difference, I suppose...Like I said, officer, get on the horn to your lieutenant. She'll put you straight."

Maass snorted and lumbered toward the kids.

"I don't care who you're related to, or how," he told them. "You're comin' with me."

As he reached for Kim, Mac stepped in front of the big cop. Maass purpled and turned – determined to pound him into dust. Then a commanding voice whipped out, freezing him in place.

"Goddamn it, Maass. Are you fucking with the public again?"

Maass jolted around to see his boss, Lieutenant Donna Snow, getting out of her plainclothes car. Snow was a weary-looking cop about Mac's age. She was a tall woman with a trim, muscular figure that didn't need much decoration. Her clothes were conservative civilian, shoes plain with just a little lift in the heels, purse utilitarian leather with a gun bulge in it, eyes and hair dark and big, plain gold hoops in her ears.

She also scared the shit out of Maass and all the other cops on the force. The rest of the officers stepped back a few paces to let Maass take the heat.

"I wasn't fuckin' with anybody, Lt. Snow," Maass said. "This guy's a lyin' sack."

Mac laughed. "You know what they say about Boca Raton," he said. "Tell a lie at breakfast, it'll be true by dinner."

Maass saw no humor in it. He raised an indignant finger and jabbed it at Mac, so there would be no way Snow could miss which lyin' sack he was talking about.

"This asshole says he's cousin to the black kid..." he said, voice shaking with emotion. Then he pointed a thick finger at Kim, who shrank back as if it were a weapon. "And the blonde bimbo. He says she's his cousin, too."

Allan Cole

Lt. Snow sighed. "They probably are his cousins, Officer Maass," she said. "Mac, here, is cousin to just about everybody who's a native of Florida--black, white, Latino and everything in between. Hell, if you weren't just down from Jersey, he'd probably be your cousin, too." She pointed at the big cop's gun. "Now, put your weapon away, Maass, so you can meet the best friend the Boca police ever had."

She made a slight gesture with her hand—almost but not quite a flourish. "You're looking at none other than Addison Mizner Flagler Titus Broward MacGregor," she said, then grinned at Mac. "Did I leave anybody out."

He shrugged. "Gomez…maybe a couple of others."

"Gomez. Right. The pirate." She turned back to Maass. "Most folks call him Mac. And we leave him the hell alone unless we catch him buggering the mayor's Chihuahua."

Mac laughed. "He still have that thing?"

Lt. Snow nodded. "Pisses on my ankle every chance it gets."

He grimaced. "Cute cyclashes, though."

Snow chuckled. Maass, however, continued fuming.

"Nice to see everything's so cozy," he said. "But I still got a problem with these two. Broke about every traffic law on the books." He indicated Kim. "Plus that one's drunk. And probably high on illegal drugs to boot."

Snow gave Mac a look. He raised a hand, palm up.

"It's like this, lieutenant," he said. "Jean's dad is the new ambassador to Brazil. Kim's mom is doing something similar in Portugal. And, well, the kids got in over their heads with the wrong crowd and the wrong inducements. Long story short, their folks came to me for help, and I'm getting them checked into rehab tomorrow." He gave his head a sad shake. "Except little Kim, there, screwed up the schedule. I'll have to get her cleaned out for another twenty-four hours before the guys at rehab will accept her."

Maass snorted derisively.

"Ambassadors?" he scoffed. "Both of them? Give me a friggin' break."

"I come from a long line of ambassadors," Mac said. Amusement twisted his lips. "And more Florida crooks than you can shake a coonskin at. A thieving governor. A crooked railroad man. The king cracker of the cattlemen. And even a few honest folks who made no bones about being outright thieves, whores and cutthroats."

Lt. Snow nodded agreement. She told Maass, "Hell, his great-uncle—man named Addison Mizner—built this town right on top of a swamp. Made a fortune selling land to dumb Yankees like you."

Maass finally realized he was licked.

"Sorry about the trouble, Mr. MacGregor," he said, but he shot the lieutenant a dirty look.

Mac gestured--no big deal.

Snow did some subtle internal gear-shifting and, with body language alone, managed to get the idea across to Maass and the others to back off.

When they were out of earshot, she said, "Haven't seen you around lately, Mackie."

He shrugged. "Yeah, I know."

"How's Barbara?"

Mac felt his mouth go dry. "Same as always," he said, voice rough. "Not good."

Snow gave a sad shake of her head.

"Life's a funny old bitch, you know?" She touched his arm in sympathy, letting it linger a little longer than mere friendship might permit. "See you later, Mac."

She left, taking the other cops with her. As the last patrol car backed out of the driveway, Kim gave a little moan and collapsed against his shoulder.

"I'm sorry, Uncle Mac," Jean said. "She wouldn't listen."

"At least you got her home, son," Mac said. "Now, let's get her to bed."

Kim sagged as if props had been kicked out from beneath her. He caught her shoulders and Jean her legs, and the two of them carried her awkwardly through the gate.

18

Allan Cole

CHAPTER FOUR

KIDS LOOKED UP from their games when the old school bus lumbered across the bridge and turned onto Orinoco Street.

The bus was a familiar sight. It was painted white, with big red crosses on each side framing signs that read Angelside Children's Clinic. A loudspeaker mounted on the roof played the Barney song both in English and Spanish.

The bus maneuvered slowly down the street – a working class neighborhood just within the northwest border of Boca. Barely claimed by the city, the neighborhood hugged a broad canal – a deep ditch, really – that swallowed wayward cars and drunks and gave back catfish and oily crabs and turtles in return.

Huge iguanas, some as long as five feet, grazed the weedy banks, to the delight of some of the transplanted islanders who caught them in traps and roasted their thick tails. The canal was a far cry from the grand river in Venezuela for which both it and the street were named.

Small homes and apartment buildings were interspersed with shops and businesses that displayed signs in Spanish, French, and English. Men and women of every variety and race tended push carts offering everything from iced mangoes to used clothing.

The kids shouted to one another as the bus went by, and some of them fell in behind to follow Barney's sugary Pied Piper song.

On board, Tampa glared out at the scene with red-rimmed eyes. He was hung over and disgusted at being up so early in the day. Bonita didn't like morning drinkers, so he was suffering from a lack of his usual medical assistance-- tomato juice and beer.

In the jumpseat beside him, Bonita smiled and waved at some of the kids. She was wearing a starched white nurse's uniform with a short skirt that showed off her fine legs, and sturdy white shoes on her trim feet. There was a colorful brochure spread across her lap.

Tampa also wore white--the open-collared shirt and trousers of an ambulance driver; he'd kept his old brown leather scrub boots. He was a Panhandle boy who favored boots and overalls dotted with IHOP syrup. Bonita had been civilizing him to the point that the overalls had first been washed, then banished to the closet. The boots, he feared, were next. So he clung to them fiercely, knowing it was a losing battle.

Bonita said, "Be nice today, Tampa. If we're lucky maybe we can make up the five hundred dollars."

Tampa did his best to act contrite.

"I'm sorry, Bonita, honey bun," he said. "She just shouldn't have bit me, you know? I can take almost anythin' but that sort of lowdown disrespect."

Bonita put on her cheeriest face. "I understand, sweetie pie," she said. "But if we're ever gonna cash in on our dreams, we've gotta really buckle down. We're not gettin' any younger, you know?" She tapped the brochure on her lap. "This RV park we bought is a real opportunity, hon. I realize it's kinda rundown. But with a little money and a whole lotta elbow grease…Well, we'll finally get our piece of the American dream just like everybody else."

"I know, baby," Tampa said. "I promised I'd turn over a new leaf and danged if I didn't."

In Tampa's mind, this was a mighty truth. Hells' bells, six months ago he'd been rollin' drunks down in the Keys. Then he got lucky enough to hook up Bonita. Now he was the bona-fide co-owner of a by God RV park, thanks to their hard work, plus knockin' over that bodega she used to do book-keepin' for.

Bonita gave him a loving smile, then went back to perusing the brochure. She turned to a foldout of a large

Allan Cole

Winnebago with a pop-out living room and an awning arched over a portable barbecue. A handsome man wearing a chef's hat and an apron tended burgers, while his perky wife, wearing a nice halter top and shorts, served drinks to guests.

Bonita sighed and wiped a bit of moisture from one eye. What she wanted more than anything in the world – now that she had Tampa - was a nice RV of their own. Why, they'd been floppin' at that fishing camp motel so long the mosquitoes know her by her first name. She was awful tired of smelling like DEET all the time. And here they had themselves a nice, mosquito-free RV park, but no RV of their own.

She showed Tampa the picture. "Look at this one, baby," she said. "Brochure says it'd make an ideal owner's unit. That's us, hon - owners."

Tampa glanced at the brochure, then took in the look pure longing on his sweetie's face. He took a resolute grip of the wheel and set his jaw. Be damned to his hangover, this is what Bonita wanted. And was she, or was she not, the woman of his dreams? A woman who put all the ones he'd met in his whole life to shame?

"Okay, sweetie pie," he said. "I'll be good. We'll get back that five hundred bucks and then some. And that's a promise."

Bonita gave him a look of great affection. "I love you, honey bunch," she said, her voice quivering with emotion.

"Me, too, hon," Tampa said, voice cracking.

It was his turn to wipe his eyes. He thought it was just plain remarkable that a smart, sophisticated woman like Bonita should love a dumb cracker like himself.

Bonita glanced out the window and saw a mass of kids gathered at the corner.

"Here we go," she said, pointing at the corner. "Pull over, baby, it's sucker time."

"What a gal," Tampa laughed, pulling over to the curb, hangover gone.

Bonita unhooked a microphone, chopped the Barney music, and keyed the mike.

"Okay, kids," she said, her voice crackling through the loudspeaker. "Angelside Clinic is now open for business. Everybody line up. And take it easy, okay? There's plenty of goodies for everybody."

She replaced the mike, and Tampa yanked the lever that opened the door. Bonita grabbed a large white briefcase with a red cross emblazoned on it and stepped off the bus, ready for business.

Outside, children and their mothers and aunts crowded around, chattering happily as Bonita handed out candy from the briefcase. Behind her, Tampa lugged a bright red scooter off the bus, and the kids all gasped in amazement as the sun sparkled off the chrome handlebars and wheels. It was the very latest, hippest Razor Scooter in the entire TVland world, and they were totally and completely in toy love.

No one more so than Leslie, Stormy's granddaughter, who stepped out of the crowd, munching free candy, her eyes aglow as she examined the scooter.

"You-all know how this deal works," Bonita said to the women. "We're gonna take the kids to the Angelside Clinic where they'll get their shots and have their teeth fixed."

She motioned to one woman, Marita Morales, an attractively exotic mixture of Hispanic and Haitian, to come forward. "Remind them about our program, Marita. Tell them how it works."

Marita beamed. A paid shill for Angelside, she turned to the crowd of women and gave a speech that would have made Avon executives weep, moving from French, to Spanish, to English and back again.

"This is for the health of our children, my dear sisters," she said. "We must all give thanks to the Blessed Virgin above who looks out for us and sends us so many kindnesses that we have such a great opportunity to guarantee our children a long and healthy life."

At this point, Bonita broke in. "And it's all for free, ladies. Free. Paid for by the good folks at the State Of Florida Board Of Health. All you ladies have to do is sign some permission slips and as a reward for your cooperation, we'll

22

Allan Cole

give each and every one of you vouchers worth ten dollars at the Rico Market."

Bonita showed them the vouchers, then handed them to Marita to pass out. The women crowded around, clamoring to sign and get their ten bucks worth of goodies.

"Wait a second, ladies," Bonita admonished them. "We're offering' an even bigger surprise." She pointed at the scooter Tampa was holding. "When we bring the boys and girls back here this afternoon we're going to have a drawing for this fantastic Razor Scooter."

Leslie and the other kids let out loud cheers at this news. They'd all been wondering if that two-wheeled marvel might by some miracle end up in their neighborhood. Kids ran off down the street to collect missing brothers and sisters so they could get in on the action. Marita raced through the crowd, snapping up permission slips, and returning them to Bonita faster than lightning from a clear Florida sky. Soon, the two women were handing out vouchers to an ever-thickening crowd. Finally, Bonita was getting down to the end. She nodded at Tampa, who started getting the kids on the bus.

"Okay, kids, all aboard," Bonita urged the stragglers. "If we're late, there won't be time to draw for the scooter."

"Yes, yes, hurry children," Marita cried, shepherding the kids on board.

This goosed the stragglers into action and in a few moments they were all on board – except for Leslie. Bonita's sharp eyes spotted the way the little girl was hanging back all teary-eyed.

"What's the matter, honey?" Bonita asked. "Isn't your momma here to sign a permission slip?"

Leslie sadly shook her head, no.

Bonita gave a meaningful look to Marita, who pressed in, her features as compassionate as the portrait of the Madonna and Child on her bedroom wall. The same bedroom where she serviced a steady stream of working men at all hours of the day and night.

"It's okay, my azucarita – my little sugar," Marita crooned. "This is important for you. For your health. I'll tell your grandmother about it. Stormy won't be mad, I promise you."

Even so, Leslie hesitated. But Bonita knew when she had the sale. She gently took Leslie's hand and led her to the bus. Although she thought about holding back, Leslie did not resist the firm adult hand, especially with Marita calling out words of encouragement.

Bonita added the capper: "Don't you worry, sweetie," she said. "We can make an exception to the rules for a pretty little girl like you."

She gave Tampa a meaningful look. "Tampa, I want you to take special care of this little girl. She's all by her lonesome."

Tampa got her drift and smiled broadly. "Don't you worry, kid," he said to Leslie as he helped her up the stairs and into a seat. "We ain't gonna let you miss out on a thing."

Bonita boarded the bus and the doors closed. The bus gave a chuff, belched black smoke, and started off down the street, the Barney song echoing across the neighborhood.

As the bus neared the corner a frantic Stormy came running up, looking wildly around. "Has anybody seen my Leslie?" she asked the mothers.

Marita pointed at the bus, which was turning the corner. "Do not worry, old woman. She went with the other children."

Stormy freaked at this news. "Why didn't you stop her?" she demanded. "I didn't give nobody permission to take my Leslie."

Marita said, "Everybody feels sorry for little Leslie. She has no mother to care for her. Just an old woman with tattoos. It's for her health, you know?"

The other women chattered agreement, rolling their eyes and starting away.

Stormy grabbed at Marita's sleeve. "When are those sons of bitches coming back?" she demanded. "Can you at least tell me that?"

Very coldly, Marita unhooked Stormy's fingers. "Five thirty, I think," she said.

24

Allan Cole

Stormy blew high and wide. "Jesus Christ, you ignorant bitches," she shouted. "Don't you know that clinic is a god damned mother humpin' rip-off?"

But no one was listening. Marita and the other women faded away, leaving Stormy to fume helplessly.

CHAPTER FIVE

THE TEENAGE GIRL was pale and silent, a slave to the
hissing machines that kept her alive. Wires and tubes ran
from her body to plastic bags and bottles that carried
nourishment in and waste out. Green lines ran their jagged
course across monitor screens, showing her vital signs.

Mac bent down, brushed dark hair away from her
forehead and kissed her.

"Hello, sweetheart," he whispered. "Daddy's here."

The girl did not--could--not reply. Mac turned to Kim,
who stood in the doorway of the intensive care unit, weeping.

"Kim," he said, "say hello to your cousin Barbara."

Kim advanced into the room.

"Hello, Barbara," she said in a shaky voice. She looked
at Mac. "Can she hear me?"

"I don't know if she can or not," Mac said. "But I talk to
her anyway. Just in case."

Kim nodded and turned back to the comatose girl.

"This is Kim, Barbara," she said. "Maybe you remember
me. I was the one who fell on your birthday cake."

She looked at Mac again.

"We were six," she said, "and I was jealous and wanted
to blow out the candles and steal her wish." She angrily
swiped at her eyes. "But I fell in the cake
instead...and...and..." She turned away from the bed,
crying. "Oh, God, I hate this. I swore I wasn't going to let
you pull any scared straight shit on me. But...But..." She
regained control. "How did it happen?" she asked. "Was she,
like, high?"

"No. But the kids in the other car were."

"Oh," Kim said, voice flat. Then: "Did they, like, go to
jail or something."

Mac sighed. "No," he said. "They died."

Kim jerked, as if stung by a wasp.

"Oh, God," she said. She took a few deep breaths. "Is Barbara really…you know…?" She couldn't get the question out.

"For all intents and purposes," Mac said, "she's dead. The machines are keeping her body alive. But there's no brain function."

Kim shuddered. "If that ever happens to me," she said, "I hope they turn the machines off."

"That's how I feel," Mac said. "And that's what Barbara would probably want. But her mom and I have different ideas, and since her mom has custody, I don't have a say in the matter."

Kim was confused. "But…you still come and visit her? Even though you don't believe…" She trailed off.

Mac gave a small smile. "It's the Irish in me," he said. "We're funny that way."

Kim laughed nervously. "Boy, do I."

She stood there awkwardly, not knowing what to do or say. Mac reached in his back pocket and pulled out a book.

"Can you give us a few minutes?"

"Sure, Uncle Mac," Kim said, relieved. "I'll meet you in the cafeteria.

She kissed him on the cheek and left. Mac pulled a chair up beside the bed and opened the book.

For a moment, Kim stepped back in. She opened her mouth to speak but stopped when she saw him with a book that bore an all-too familiar cover. It was Anna Sewell's Black Beauty: The Autobiography Of A Horse.

Mac started to read. "'The first place I can well remember was a large pleasant meadow with a pond of clear water in it…'"

Kim stood very still, listening. Tears streamed down her face.

CHAPTER SIX

THE ANGELSIDE CHILDREN'S Clinic was a long, two-story building shot with Florida-pink stucco and set in the middle of a large blacktop parking lot that was surrounded by a high chain link fence. The fact that the fence was topped with three rows of razor wire and the only entrance was a guarded gate belied its angelic claims, if not its appeal for children.

Even so, the kids poured off Tampa's bus shouting and cheering as if they were going to Disneyland. Seedy-looking men and women dressed in badly washed hospital whites and with false smiles pasted on their faces and sweet stuff in their paws escorted the kids through the main doors of the clinic. It was like a scene out of Pinocchio, except in this case most of the kids were familiar with the painless, well-rewarded routine.

They'd be hustled through some cursory dental exams, which included X-rays, and their gums and teeth would be briefly scrubbed with industrial-strength mouthwash. Then they'd be treated to hotdogs and baked beans before being rushed through a fast physical, where marks would be put on charts for nonexistent infirmities that were logged as treated, even though they were not. Real problems were ignored, because who had time for them?

Afterward, the kids would be let loose in a vast playland of arcade games and videos and cartoons while the staff entered their ailments, their treatments and the costs incurred into computers which were tied directly into the State Of Florida's Children's Authority Offices. Separate hard-copy printouts of each child's records and his/her transaction were made so they could be mailed in thick manila envelopes to the same authority.

Although the Angelside administrators complained about the extra effort and cost, they did it efficiently, because this new hard-copy requirement was the result of a fraud investigation launched the previous year after a series of articles in the Miami Herald. Angelside had missed an indictment by a whisker of a bribed assistant DA's moustache.

At day's end the children were sent home none the worse for wear--other than a few more x-ray rads and the neglect of the truly sick--to play happily in the street until the next time the big white bus showed up. Meanwhile, their mothers gratefully spent the ten-dollar vouchers at the Rico Market, supplementing the family food budget with a few extra treats.

It was a lovely Florida scam, an old Florida scam in a state well-known for scams. But only recently had the scam stretched into new territory--the dark side of Pinocchio's dream.

It played out like this.

As the kids hopped off the bus, Bonita stood beside the doorway, ostensibly helping each one. Actually she was counting them--one, two, three; and while she counted, Ed Rollins, a big man in hospital whites and a superior air stood beside her, putting bills into her hand. He was counting in twenties: three-forty...three-sixty...three-eighty. And while he counted, Tampa stood on the other side, a sneer on his face and a suspicious look in his eye.

When Rollins reached three-eighty, the flow of kids stopped. Frowning, he looked up and saw Leslie's sad face staring out at him from the window. She was still in her seat.

"What about her?" he asked, reasonably enough. "Make it an even four hundred."

Bonita said, "No, thanks. We're taking her directly to Mr. Novarro."

Rollins displayed chemically whitened teeth.

"The boss will be glad to hear that," he said. "He's still a little pissed about you guys losing one in the swamp."

Tampa boiled in, his pride injured to the quick.

"Hold it right there, Rollins," he snarled. "We didn't lose nothin'. I know right where that little bitch is--"

"Never you mind, sweetie pie," Bonita broke in, trying her best to avoid a controversial topic.

Tampa was in no mood to avoid controversy--not with his reputation being impugned.

"But I do mind, hon," he said. "I know right where I buried her. I resent folks sayin' I lost somethin' when I didn't...you know?"

Bonita knew. "Sure, baby," she said. "Just like Mr. Rollins don't mean nothing by it." She gave Rollins a shot of daggers from under her long Spanish lashes. "Do you, Mr. Rollins...sir?"

Rollins hastily made his peace. Tampa spooked him, but Bonita scared holy hell out of him. She was not a woman to be messed with.

"No, no. Not at all, Bonita." He smiled at Tampa. "I'll tell Mr. Novarro you're on your way with another five hundred-dollar package."

Tampa liked that and grinned hugely at Bonita, as if to say: See, I kept my promise, right, hon? Bonita had always been partial to his smiles, which she thought made him look like a mischievous little boy and it made her heart go pitter-pat.

But she kept to business.

"Listen," she said to Rollins, "we're going to be super busy with Mr. Novarro, so you gotta get somebody else to drive those kids home." She counted back forty dollars from her stash, offering it to Rollins.

He nodded. "No problem," he said. "For forty bucks Williams will be happy to take care of it."

Bonita thanked him, caught Tampa's arm and nudged him up the steps of the bus before something else happened.

As they climbed on board, Bonita noticed that Leslie was looking worried. After all, she was the only kid left on the bus. Besides, Bonita guessed, the kid probably had to pee. She'd get Tampa to stop in a bit and let the kid use the little girls' room, buy her some ice cream, or some such.

Allan Cole

The girl looked at Bonita with pleading eyes. "Don't I get to go too?" she asked with a bit of a sob. "I might not get a chance at the scooter if I don't."

Bonita gave her a hug and a big kiss on the cheek. "Honey, don't you worry your pretty little head about one thing," she said. "See, honey pie, you just advanced to the next level. Never mind those kids. You're gonna get the bestest scooter in the whole blamed world and your grandmother's gonna be so proud of you, just you wait and see."

Leslie looked enthralled. "Really?" she asked.

Bonita laughed and gave her another kiss. "Would I lie to a pretty little thing like you?" she said.

Tampa laughed uproariously, shoved the bus into gear and rumbled away.

*   *   *

At five-thirty, Stormy waited impatiently on Orinoco Street as the white bus rumbled and coughed its way across the bridge into the neighborhood. She anxiously scanned the windows for Leslie's face, her heart bumping harder as each child she saw turned out to be somebody else.

At the corner, the bus pulled up with a squeal of its rusty brakes, the doors came open and all the women crowded around to collect their children. Stormy pushed her way forward through laughing kids, crying kids, arguing kids-- they were all tired and hyped on Angelside sugar--to get to the open doors.

The panic in her breast grew as the kids emerged one-by-one and still no Leslie. Finally the last kid got off and the driver, a black guy with a tag on his shirt that read, Williams, handed Marita the scooter for the promised lottery, then climbed back on and started to shut the doors.

Stormy grabbed the edge of one door and forced it back open.

"Hey," Williams shouted. "Whatcha doin'?"

"Where's my grandkid?" she demanded. "Where's my Leslie?"

Williams shook his head. "I don't know about no Leslie," he said. "I just pick 'em up and put 'em down, lady. That's my job."

Once again, he hit the lever that closed the doors.

Stormy's temper erupted. She gripped the edges of both doors with her fingertips and, as small as she was, slowly forced them apart, like a circus strongwoman bending iron bars. The tattoos leaped and squirmed on her arms and neck as she strained and strained, until finally, there was a crack! and the doors sprang open.

Alarmed, Williams jumped to his feet and tried to muscle them shut. He couldn't believe someone so small could be so strong.

"Get away, you crazy-ass skank," he cried.

"You dirty sons of bitches," Stormy shouted. "I want my Leslie and I want her now."

"Go away, go away, before I call the cops," was Williams weak retort as he struggled with the door.

"You better watch out," Stormy warned him. "Ask anybody around here. Stormy Nichols is not to be fucked with. Even Hell's Angels don't mess with me."

Williams gave it all he had--one more mighty shove-- and the doors closed. Immediately, he threw himself into the driver's seat, slammed the bus into gear and tore out of there as fast as a twenty-year-old, beat-up, out of tune school bus could go.

Stormy fell to the ground, weeping in frustration and filling the air with terrible curses.

Marita and the other women looked at her, crossed themselves, then hurried away to leave her to her torment.

Allan Cole

CHAPTER SEVEN

THROUGH HIS BINOCULARS, Angel Novarro watched Tampa and Bonita approach on their airboat. A child sat in the bow, trailing her fingers in the lake water.

"Excellent, Senor Hanson," he said. "They're bringing another one. A girl, I believe." He spoke with a soft Spanish accent.

Novarro was in his late forties and kept himself fit. From the neck down he looked good in his expensive tropical suit. From the neck up he looked a lot like former Panamanian dictator Manuel Noriega, or a member of some South American death squad, with his stomped-on face, greased-back hair and heavy eyebrows.

He offered his companion the binoculars. Hanson took them and gave a bored peek at the airboat's progress. He was a big man--a little too muscular for his Ivy League superiors at the CIA. They suspected him of taking steroids, which he did. Also, he favored loud shirts, baggy khaki shorts and leather sandals, a no-no in the buttoned down world of Langley.

"We should be close to our quota," Novarro said, "should we not?"

"That one's a replacement, Mr. Novarro," Hanson reminded him. "Remember?"

Novarro nodded. "Oh, yes," he said. "For the child who suffered that unfortunate accident. Such a pity. I don't know why it is so, but the death of a child seems more tragic than others, don't you agree?"

Hanson shrugged. "You know what they say--only the young die good."

Novarro's eyes widened; he was impressed.

"That's most profound," he said. "I must remember that. 'Only the young die good.'" He laughed. "I suppose that means you and I will live forever, Senor Hanson." He snorted amusement. "So many sins. So little time." He beckoned to Hanson. "Come. I must see to the other children."

The two men walked toward a long boathouse that jutted out from the overgrown shoreline. A Humvee was parked outside the main door, and several tough-looking men lounged around two truckloads of supplies, smoking cigarettes and shooting the bull.

Novarro snapped his fingers at them. "Hurry up, you lazy asses," he said. "I have polo practice this afternoon."

The men quickly got back to unloading the trucks.

"The opening match of the season is almost upon us," he told Hanson. "My team is fortunate enough to be the defending champion."

"That so?" Hanson said, pretending interest. "Well, good luck, then."

Novarro chuckled. "No luck involved, senor," he said. "I have already taken out some--shall we say--insurance."

Hanson's eyebrows crawled upward. This was more up his alley.

"Insurance, huh?" he said. "You mean like the competition breaks some bones kind of insurance?"

Novarro grinned. "How well you know me, Senor Hanson," he said.

Two men slid aside the big doors, and Novarro and Hanson strolled into the boathouse. Several large speedboats were tied up in their berths, bobbing in the lake water. A long, rickety stairway led up to the second story. Novarro and Hanson headed for the stairs.

"What about the child who died?" Novarro asked. "I hope that little incident won't endanger our plans."

Hanson was quick to reassure him. "I double checked just in case," he said. "Her mom and big brother made some noise when she first went missing. But they got deported, thanks to our pals at the INS. Which made her just like the others we got stashed upstairs - no family, no friends, or anybody else who gives a damn." He shrugged. "If they ever

34

Allan Cole

find the body, it'll be one more Juanita Doe for the morgue students to practice on."

Novarro sighed. "Even so, it was a pity we had to waste all those youthful parts," he said. "I have clients who would have paid a hundred-thousand dollars for the eyes alone."

Hanson rolled his big shoulders. "We didn't have time to get the corpse on ice, much less the facilities or personnel to operate. You know how it is in this climate."

They reached the stairs and started climbing.

"Besides," Hanson went on, "the Agency wants to keep this totally deniable. Which means everything has to happen out of the country."

Novarro smiled. "Most amusing," he said, "to think we are providing the Agency the ultimate bribe for the tyrants of the world. Eat, drink, fuck all you want, and when it comes time to replace your worn-out lungs or kidneys, all you have to do is contact Angel Novarro and his CIA friends. We will provide you eternal youth in return for your obedience."

They reached the top of the stairs and paused.

"I have to admit, Mr. Novarro," Hanson said, "that, diplomatically, this is probably the first truly genius idea of the new century. Gives the whole 'arms for hostages' concept a brand new meaning, doesn't it?"

The guards opened the doors at the top of the stairs, and Novarro put a finger to his lips, urging Hanson to be quiet. Hanson nodded and whispered, "Don't want to mess with their beauty sleep."

They entered a long dorm room painted hospital white, with bars on the curtained windows. Fly fans spun overhead, sending a soft breeze over row after row of children sleeping in iron cots. White-coated techs moved along the rows, checking the kids.

Supervising the room was Rosa Cortez, a stern, muscular woman in a starched nurse's uniform. When the men entered, she hurried over to them, support stockings whisking as her sturdy thighs brushed together.

Novarro looked around and nodded his approval.

"Everything looks quite in order, Mrs. Cortez," he said.

"Thank you, Senor Novarro," she said briskly. "We had to make a few adjustments when Marie escaped, but I'm sure that will never happen again."

Hanson lifted an eyebrow, his professional interest aroused.

"What precautions did you take?" he asked.

"Prior to the escape," Mrs. Cortez said, "we put the sedatives in the food. Marie was a bright little girl and thought it through enough to starve herself so she could flee. Now, instead of putting it in their food, we give them all injections." She shrugged. "The little ones cry, but I give them a lollipop and say, 'It's just a pinch, my dear.'"

Novarro nodded his approval. Then they heard footsteps approach, and the shrill voice of a complaining child demanded, "What is this place?"

* * *

Bonita and Tampa entered, Leslie between them. Immediately, Leslie spotted the rows of unconscious children.

"What's wrong with those kids?" she asked, alarmed.

Panic set in and she turned to run, but Tampa grabbed her. She shouted for him to let go, and the children in the cots stirred in their sleep. She kicked him in the shins, and once again he started to lose it. His face purpled with rage, and he grabbed the child by the shoulders and shook her violently.

Everyone was frozen in shock for a moment, but Mrs. Cortez swiftly intervened.

"Stop that, young man," she snapped. "That's valuable merchandise."

Tampa was jolted by her commanding voice, and he let the child go. Bonita pulled him aside, whispering soothing things to him, calming him down. Meanwhile, Mrs. Cortez put an arm around Leslie, and the child pressed against her, seeking safety.

The woman motioned to one of her techs, who approached with a hypodermic. Then she leaned down and stroked Leslie's head.

Allan Cole

"The doctor said you needed some medicine," she said soothingly.

She fetched a lollipop from her pocket, offering it to Leslie. The girl gave a fearful smile, but she unpeeled the candy and put it into her mouth.

"You be a good girl, my darling," Mrs. Cortez said. "All you'll feel is a pinch."

Leslie stood quietly, eyes wide, sucking on her lollipop, as the tech gave her the shot. She didn't even flinch when the needle went in.

"What a brave little girl you are, sweetheart," Mrs. Cortez murmured, wiping away a tiny drop of blood with an alcohol swatch and putting a small Band-Aid on the spot. There was a picture of the Cookie Monster on the Band-Aid.

"That's the way to do it," Novarro said with evident satisfaction. "Very professional."

All of a sudden Leslie moaned and collapsed to the floor. Mrs. Cortez and the tech knelt beside her, checking her vital signs.

"She's not breathing," the tech said, his voice borderline panicking.

"What's wrong?" Hanson demanded. "What's happening?"

"I don't know," Mrs. Cortez said. "A bad reaction to the medicine, perhaps."

"Well, do something," Novarro snapped. "There's a great deal of money riding on that girl."

Mrs. Cortez didn't reply. She was already frantically at work over Leslie, giving her CPR and massaging her chest.

Tampa gave Bonita a meaningful look. She could tell what he was thinking. They'd done their job and had five hundred coming to them whether the kid lived or not.

She gave his hand a squeeze.

"It'll be fine, hon," she whispered as the child thrashed about on the floor. "Puts us over the hump for a down on the RV."

CHAPTER EIGHT

STORMY AIMED HER battered pickup at the closed gates of the Angelside Children's Clinic. A uniformed guard ran out of the shack and raised a hand for her to stop. This only caused her to floor it, and the guard leaped out of the way just in time.

She crashed through the gate, continued on to the front of the clinic and screeched to a halt. She kicked the door open and hopped out. The gate guard started running toward her but came to a fast stop when he saw her turn and lift a pump-action shotgun off the front seat of the pickup.

Stormy pumped a round into the chamber then fired a blast into the air.

"Send out my granddaughter," she shouted, firing again for emphasis. "If I don't see my Leslie out here in five seconds I'm gonna blow shit out of this place."

Then she started counting. "One...two...three...four..."

She opened up, blowing out windows, glass doors, firing round after round into the building.

Off in the distance there was a wail of many, many police cars. Stormy blazed away.

*****

It was night before a red-faced jailer named Charlie Fisher escorted Mac to the holding cell where Stormy paced like an underfed, tattooed leopard. When she spotted Mac she rushed to the bars.

"Thank friggin' God you came," she cried. "I can't find out what the hell they did with my Leslie."

"Hold on, Stormy," Mac said. "First, let's get this show on the road. Then you can tell me what's going on." He motioned to the jailer. "Can you help us out here, Charlie?" he asked. "I posted bail and I'm waiting for the release form to hit."

"Sure, Mac, no problem," Charlie said. He checked his watch. "I'm off in ten. If the release takes longer than that, I'll give Sam a heads-up."

Mac thanked him, and Charlie opened the door and let him in. Stormy ran to Mac, who embraced her, holding her until she was calm. Finally, Stormy pushed away and gave her wet eyes an angry swipe.

"I hate to cry," she said. Her temper flared. "Hate it. Hate it." She took a deep breath, getting herself together. She looked up at Mac. "They grabbed my Leslie, Mac," she said. "And they won't give her back."

"I called the clinic," Mac informed her. "They claimed she was never admitted."

"Bullshit. She got on that bus. I've got witnesses."

Mac said nothing, waiting until realization sank in. Stormy groaned.

"God damn, I don't have shit, do I? None of those women will talk to the law. Jesus Christ, what am I gonna do?"

"When I was checking around," Mac said, "I heard some funny business about Angelside--phony treatments, phony bills. But nobody said anything about kidnapping."

Stormy snorted. "It's white slavery, that's what."

Mac lifted an eyebrow. "Come on, Stormy. In this day and age?"

She shrugged. "I'm the poster child for that shit, Mac. You know that. My mother sold me to a motorcycle gang when I was a baby. Just about everythin' that can happen to a body happened to me after that. Up to and includin' bein' a crack whore." She dragged a hand over the tattoos on her arms. "That's how I wound up with this garbage all over me."

Mac smiled. "When I was looking for a housekeeper, a good friend mentioned your name. Said you were as honest and hardworking as they come. But she warned me first-- 'Don't mind the tattoos,' she said. And I've never regretted taking that advice."

"You've been good to me, Mac," Stormy said. "And good to Leslie, too. No tellin' where her momma is. Heard she was dead, but I don't know for certain. My poor Debbie never did recover from bein' my kid. It's my fault and I know it. But I can't take that back." Her voice broke, and she struggled for control. "So the least I can do is take care of Leslie, you know?"

"I know," Mac said, as gently as he could.

Stormy took several deep breaths. Finally, she got up the nerve to ask: "Although you never came right out and told me what you do for a livin', Mac, I got the general idea sometimes it involves nasty stuff. Stuff other guys are scared to touch."

He shrugged. "I fix things, is all. Kind of a handyman for people in bad trouble."

Stormy gripped his arm. "Well, Mac, as sure as my soul is damned to hell for all eternity, I am in bad trouble. And I need your help in the worst way. Nothin' I can do to repay you. I don't have a mother-humpin' cent to my name. But if you ever need a friend, Mac, for anythin' up to and includin' blowin' some son of a bitch away, no questions asked, just call on me."

"I don't often need the services of an assassin, Stormy," Mac said dryly. "But if I ever do…"

Enormous relief washed over Stormy. She sagged back on the cot, and tears started to flow.

"God damn it to hell, Mac," she said. "What must you think of me? There I go leakin' tears again. Shit, shit, shit."

Allan Cole

CHAPTER NINE

ABOUT A HUNDRED yards short of the sign that promised fishermen and campers that Lake Okeechobee was only ten miles ahead, Mac turned the Jeep off the highway onto a country road. It was tarmac for about a mile, running between two bottomless Florida ditches notorious for devouring drunk drivers on moonless nights.

Mac didn't have a lighting problem as he steered the Jeep down the track. It was just dusk, the setting sun sending red rays across the swamp, illuminating a barefoot boy fishing in the shadow of a mossy oak. For just a second he remembered what it was like when he was boy with not a serious thought in his head, except maybe if a mouse was really better than a frog to bait a bigmouth bass.

The Jeep crunched over gravel, then a tractor-rutted track that ran through farmland reclaimed from swamp. It had rained recently, and steam rose from row after row of yellow squash, broad leaves straining wide to catch the dying rays of the sun. In other areas there were teepees of runner beans, colonies of Big Boy tomatoes, melon patches rich and loamy and filling the air with their sweetness, all mixed in with a whole field of yellow corn so sugary on the blessed evening breeze that it made Mac's teeth ache to sink into a cob.

Developers had pushed Boca Raton deep into the farmlands that had once surrounded the beach town. In Mac's boyhood, a kid couldn't bicycle more than a mile before running into farms, with their fresh-from-the-field veggie stands; or sweet water fishing holes with makeshift docks where a boy could relax against the pilings and pitch his line. It wasn't so long ago that in the middle of Boca there were mossy oak forests so thick you could easily get lost. Now it was given over to condo developments named after the trees they replaced, like Oaks Of Boca; or mini malls, medical complexes, and the Florida Atlantic University Campus, which sprawled across many acres of what had once been a lush wilderness.

He glanced over at Stormy, who sat silently beside him, grim-faced and motionless, except for the tattoos jumping on her lean, muscular arms whenever she moved. He wished there was something he could say to comfort her, but it would most likely be a lie.

Just as he spotted the vehicles crouched around a raw, empty place in a nearby field, he saw Stormy's left bicep bunch. Her arms might have been scrawny; but her bicep stood out in stark relief, easily as big as an orange. Which was huge for a woman of her small proportions. On that bicep he saw a skull with a hypodermic rammed through its temple, grinning up at him, blood dripping on both sides.

"Is that it?" she asked, her voice quivering, stretching her arm, the skull vanishing, as she pointed.

"Think so." Mac pulled the Jeep off the track and tucked it behind a stand of trees.

It became truly night as the sun dipped below the horizon. When he shut off the engine, sounds of crickets and frogs and other nocturnal creatures seeking one another exploded into his ears. He was momentarily confused, disoriented, as he flashed back on other landings--also perilous, but on more distant shores.

Mac shook off the images as Stormy started to get out. He put a hand on that skull-decorated bicep. But he did it gently.

"Maybe you'd better wait here, Stormy. Cops can get touchy about crime scenes, you know?"

He braced for an outburst, but Stormy reacted as he'd hoped. She was oddly subdued as she turned to him.

"Oh, God, Mack What if it's Leslie?"

"Let's just take it as it goes, Stormy. Okay?"

Stormy sniffled and nodded obediently. It broke his heart. But he knew better than to touch her, or offer any kind of comfort, because she would not only snap, but hate him for being the cause of it. He handed her some DEET to ward off the mosquitoes and she dutifully splashed some on. Mac did the same and it was just in time because the stinging little bitches were already swarming around them. There'd been recent mosquito-borne problems with Nile and other dreaded diseases that neither Mac or Stormy wanted any part of.

When you live in the middle of what is basically a swampy jungle, but are surrounded by thousands of people, it is sometimes difficult to remember that all dangers might not necessarily come from your fellow man. In Boca, a wealthy person's town, a well-protected town, you were almost as likely to be mugged by a "skeeter" carrying the Nile disease, than a junkie with a knife. Sometimes gators ate poodles at the local golf courses, but that was another deal all together. Personally, Mac thought the gators had a right to all the interloping poodles they could find.

Mac exited the Jeep and gingerly made his way across the muddy field. A few cops were wrestling light stanchions into place to illuminate the area. A police photographer was stalking the scene, the flash on his camera strobing across the stark particulars of someone's final nightmare.

When he reached the gathering of vehicles and cops and technicians, Lt. Snow spotted him and came over. She was dressed for a swamp-side homicide investigation--faded jeans, rubber boots and an old khaki shirt. An ID hung on a leather thong around her neck. A light stanchion blasted on and she held up her left hand to block glare. A gold band gleamed on her ring finger.

Sometimes Mac regretted that band. He had done things in the past to assure its permanence by keeping Mr. Snow out of an orange jumpsuit. He wondered what she saw in the creep.

He gave a philosophical sigh. Snow heard the sigh, took it for impatience and flashed a smile of apology.

"Hang on a sec, Mac," she said.

She motioned to some men grouped around a muddy hole. They were zipping up a body bag that contained something pitifully small. They stopped their work, and Mac saw a ghastly little face framed by the bag.

"Over here, Mac," Snow said unnecessarily, and he followed her to the body bag.

He looked down at the mottled features of a teenage girl. Jesus, he thought, in a couple of years she would've been a heartbreaker. Then he hated himself for not wondering about the mind behind those mud-crusted eyes. Shit, she could've grown up to be a Madam Curie, or a Madeline Albright.

Ah, but who could goddamned tell with someone so young? Beautiful or brilliant. Or maybe both. Bottom line: those long, elegant fingers wrinkled by grave mud would never be accepting a beauty crown, much less the Nobel Prize.

He gave himself a mental shake. Jesus, it was always so much tougher with kids.

Mac turned to Snow and said, "It's not Leslie." Then he licked dry lips and added, "Thank God."

He immediately regretted the words. "What a lousy thing to say," he told Snow. "God shouldn't be thanked for shit like this."

He noticed her red-rimmed eyes. She looked like she'd been up around the clock. Longer than this detail had taken. Once again, he wondered about Mr. Snow. Shook that off as well. Damn, he was getting punchy.

"How'd it happen?" he asked.

Snow lifted her hand, making it into a pistol. Pointed it at her head.

"One right here," she said. "Like a drug deal gone bad. But she's no dealer. She's just a kid." She patted his arm. "Sorry for the wild goose chase, Mac."

"Don't be sorry. Just get the son of a bitch who did this thing." Then he had a thought. "Who found the grave?"

Snow smiled a bitter smile and shook her head. "Go figure," she said. "It was one of your cousins. Albert Gomez."

Mac straightened up. "Mad Albert," he said. "No kidding. What was he doing out here?"

Snow made a strained attempt at humor. "Some kind of a frog survey," she said, rolling her eyes at Albert's weird

Allan Cole

ways. "I didn't really get into it with him… There's only so much a person needs to know about frogs."

Mac allowed a small smile. "Unless you're Mad Albert."

Snow grimaced. "Unless you're Mad Albert."

She went back to her work. Yelled at the men carrying the body across the muddy field as if they'd done something wrong--like their ham-handedness had somehow caused this tragedy.

Then, like a bad prophecy waiting to follow the shout, a big razorback hog broke from a clump of bushes and ran across the field. The men nearly fell trying to avoid the animal. It had been years since Mac had seen a wild pig, and he thought about the old cracker wives' claims that a pig running across your path meant starvation, or worse. Or, perhaps in this case it was a lucky omen. Maybe, just maybe, old Florida hadn't entirely vanished into gated communities filled with retired people from Brooklyn or New Jersey.

But the moment the pig disappeared into a stand of trees the entire train of thought dissolved and his footsteps grew weary thinking about that poor damned kid as he trudged back to the Jeep.

Images of all the other dead or doomed children he'd dealt with over the years flashed through his mind. Like when he'd been a cub reporter--before the Company got into his shorts--and he'd worked an old teenage suicide. Sort of a Ross McDonald mystery—sins of the fathers—but not so classy, as it turned out.

That had been his first. Guy and his dog walking by an old abandoned spring house. Dog ducks into the rubble, growling and digging. Finds teenager missing fifteen years-- head on one side of the spring house, body on the other. Frayed old rope still hanging there in the middle.

Mom's hope that the boy--her beautiful but always so sad and out-of-place boy--had run off with the circus was put paid by that scene.

There were others. So many damned others. Kids beaten to death and buried. Kids beaten near to death, then locked into closets to die. Kids with cigarette burns because they cried. Kids with broken bones because they didn't. Brutally

45

raped kids, and children seduced by sick adults who won their trust because they were their fathers, mothers, uncles and even priests.

As for the kid in the barn, the way it worked out was that he'd been despondent because a priest had seduced that good Catholic boy. Mac wrote that story, but the paper showed it to the bishop of Miami first and so the article never saw the light of day.

A good time for a career change.

Enter the CIA.

And more kids--children in other lands brutalized in terrible ways. War victims, tribal murder victims, rape victims, exploding mine victims--just about any atrocity a sick mind could imagine had been committed against children.

All those images ran though Mac's mind as he returned to the Jeep. Then he had the depressing thought that no matter what crimes he had witnessed against children before new ones could, and would, be not only imagined but put into practice.

The mental image of his daughter's face hit him like a blow.

Barbara.

So pale.

So still.

Framed by golden hair.

She could be the fairy tale princess, waiting for the kiss of the prince to awaken her to a glad life, full of years and happiness.

But for Barbara there was only the rumbling and the groaning and the hissing of machines. Monitors showing the peaks and valleys of her life.

Dead…or not?

Suffering or…?

Barbara's face was the one that usually started—but always ended—his personal slide show of horrors. This time it had been another kid's face, streaked with blood and mud

Allan Cole

and hanging out of a body bag, that had begun the chain of mental images.

He shook himself. For Christ's sake, get it together, Mac. What'll Stormy think?

Stormy sat in the Jeep, her entire being focused on him, searching for some sign of what to expect. Before he could change his expression, he saw her mistake his haggard demeanor. A look of horror stole over her features. And pain—a terrible pain, as if a splintered stake had been driven through her heart.

He didn't waste time cursing himself for being an unfeeling jerk; he quickly gave her the thumbs-up sign. Her face beamed gladness, and over the rumble of the old coroner's wagon firing up, he heard her cry, "Oh, Jesus love me."

Then he saw her happiness collapse, realizing the same thing he had--if it wasn't Leslie, it was still some other woman's child.

"Oh, Sweet Mother Mary forgive me," she moaned. "One of your babies is bad dead."

CHAPTER TEN

THE WHITE BUS with the red crosses and Angelside Clinic sign sat in its usual spot on Orinoco Street and Barney sang his bilingual songs over the loudspeaker as the kids climbed on board. Mac and Stormy pulled up, and she saw Williams standing at the door of the bus, directing kids and handing out vouchers to their mothers.

"That's the son of a bitch," she shouted.

Mac steered the Jeep over the curb and ran right up alongside the bus. He got out, Stormy coming in from the other side, and advanced on Williams.

The driver's eyes widened when he saw them coming, but Mac could tell that what really freaked the guy out was the sight of Stormy, who was practically spitting in fury.

"The crazy broad," he shouted. "Get away, get away."

He shoved kids aside and jumped for the steps, but Mac grabbed him by the collar. Williams jerked around, swinging for all he was worth.

Mac brushed the blow aside and gave him two shots to the body, doubling him over. Williams wasn't going easy – he snaked an arm around Mac's knees and tried to throw him over. Mac clubbed him away, nearly breaking his arm.

Williams flopped over on his belly, got to his knees and scrambled up the steps of the bus. He reached under the dash.

"He's got a gun," Stormy yelled.

Williams came around, finger already tightening on the trigger. Mac grabbed his gun hand and jerked it upward. There was a loud explosion. Kids screamed, and a large hole appeared in the roof of the bus.

Mac got a better grip on the man's wrist.

"You dumb son of a bitch," he said, twisting hard.

There was an audible crack of bone breaking. Williams yelped, and Mac none too gently disarmed him, grabbed him by the collar and dragged him squealing onto the pavement.

The kids cheered and swarmed back on the bus to play. The windshield wipers flapped into life, blinkers blinked, horns honked and the doors whapped open and shut.

Mac dragged Williams a few yards away so they could talk. Stormy stood by his side, quivering with rage. To encourage the conversational flow, he lifted the driver up and gave him a swat across the chops then let him fall back again.

"What the hell you want, man?" Williams sobbed.

"I told you yesterday," Stormy growled. "I want my grandkid, Leslie."

"I don't know no Leslie, lady. I'm not even the regular driver."

"But you picked the kids up here yesterday morning, right?" Mac said. "And took them to the clinic?"

As Williams appeared to consider this statement and slowly realize he had an alibi—and a by-God honest alibi, at that - a mass of teenagers was gathering around the bus. Graffiti soon filled all that white space while the kids inside the bus shouted for a turn at the spray cans.

"Wasn't me yesterday morning," Williams finally said. "I just brung 'em back in the afternoon. Somebody else picked 'em up."

"Who?" Mac demanded.

Williams squirmed. "No skin off my nose, man," he whined. "It was Tampa and Bonita. This is their regular route, but they couldn't work yesterday afternoon. And they couldn't work today, neither. That's why I'm here."

"Where can we find them?" Mac asked.

Williams shook his head. "Beats the shit out of me, man," he said. "You gotta ask Mr. Rollins at the clinic. He's the boss."

"I'll be sure to do that." Mac shoved the guy away. "Get."

Williams got, holding his wrist in one hand as he stumbled back to the bus, which had been totally transformed by the teenagers into a work of art from gangland hell. As he neared the vehicle, one of the teenage boys on board fired up the engine. Williams stood in bewildered horror as the others cheered and rushed onto the bus. He staggered toward the folding doors, but the young driver laughed at him and jerked them shut.

With a belch of black smoke and a grinding of gears, the bus took off, lights blinking, horn sounding, kids shouting out the windows and having a grand old time. The Barney theme song was suddenly ironic.

Mac watched Williams try to chase after the bus, but he didn't manage more than half-a-dozen paces before pain made him stop. He gripped his wrist, moaning and breathing hard, then he looked up at the heavens and cried, "What'd I do, man?"

Stormy had a good laugh at that.

Allan Cole

CHAPTER ELEVEN

MEN WERE WORKING on the broken gates when Mac tooled up to the Angelside Clinic. The guard saw the Jeep and stepped out to pull them over, but when he spotted Stormy he backpedaled and grabbed for the phone.

Mac drove slowly and very deliberately through the opening between the busted metal uprights and pulled up in front of the admin building. He stopped, glanced curiously around at the boarded-up windows and glass doors then shook his head in admiration.

"You sure did a bang-up job, Stormy," he said. "They've got to give you that."

When they reached the front door, another guard was waiting. He had big arms, thick legs and a gravity defying beer belly hanging over his belt - all encased in a too-tight rent-a-cop uniform.

"We're closed," he snarled.

"Is that so?" Mac said mildly. He looked behind him at the busted gates. "You should post a sign."

*   *   *

Rollins was at his desk, the phone to his ear and a worried expression on his face.

"Okay, okay," he said. "Just calm down and don't let anybody else through the gate, understand?" He slammed down the phone.

Then he thought it best to take his own advice and started doing breathing exercises. Inhale. Exhale. Inhale. Exhale. Shake your arms and rock your head. Inhale. Exhale. Another shake…

Shouts and the sounds of scuffling interrupted his stress relief, and he snapped to, rising to his feet, abandoning the safety of his chair. Someone hollered in pain, his office door slammed open, and a guard sailed into the room, crashed against the desk and slumped to the floor. A burst of papers flew off the top, and Rollins grabbed at them, snatching one here, missing another there.

Just as he realized what a useless mission it was, there was another yell - wilder and more painful than before — and a second guard stumbled into the office, tripped over his comatose buddy and sprawled on the floor.

Then a big man in a Hawaiian shirt and faded jeans came in, brushing himself off. To Rollins' horror, he realized he was looking at none other than "Mac" MacGregor, well-known in South Florida circles for readjusting villainous attitudes and spines.

Worse still, he next spotted the little wild woman who had shot up his clinic the previous day and was apparently intent on repeating the destruction.

"You," he shouted at Stormy.

Rollins reached for his desk drawer and started to pull out a gun, but Mac got there first and knocked him back into the chair. He lifted the gun out of the drawer and examined it with a jaundiced eye.

"For a children's clinic," Mac said, "you people sure have a lot of guns around."

The second guard started to get up.

"Why don't you take a little nap until we're done here," Mac advised.

The guard sagged back down. The other didn't move at all.

Rollins tried to bluster. "I don't know what you're up to," he said, "but the police will soon sort this out."

He reached for the phone, but Mac grabbed his thumb. He squeezed slightly and Rollins felt a sharp pain race up arm. He settled down.

Mac fished a card from his shirt pocket and showed it to him.

"Try this number," he said. "It's a direct line to Lieutenant Snow of the Boca Raton PD. I think she's on her way over here anyway, with a team of auditors from the state health authorities."

Allan Cole

Rollins' heart tried to escape through his throat. He swallowed hard, then decided a little bluffing might be in order.

"Screw you," he said with far more bravery than he possessed. "I'm no fool."

"To hell with all this talk," Stormy snapped. "Where's my Leslie?"

Rollins gave it all he had. "Lady, I told you and the authorities yesterday that I don't know of any Leslie. Nor do I have a record of any child by that name."

"I understand that you're a busy man," Mac said. "Might miss the details. But what we are particularly interested in is two of your drivers. They go by the names of Tampa and Bonita."

Rollins shook his head. "I haven't the faintest—"

Mac's grabbed him by the throat and suddenly Rollins couldn't breathe. Blood hammered at his temples and he felt his face start to swell.

"A trick I learned in my salad days," Mac said. "One good squeeze and goodbye voice box. You'll be talking like Darth Vader for the rest of your life."

Desperately, Rollins tried to speak – to plead for his life, but only a croak came out.

"Think you can help us?" Mac asked, squeezing harder.

Rollins nodded furiously, and Mac let go. Rollins sucked in huge quantities of air, feeling a lot like a beached fish.

"They're… just…just…" He stopped, shook his head in frustration – he still couldn't speak - and reached for the open desk drawer.

Mac got there first, knocking his hand aside. He grinned when he saw that Rollins was only after a half-pint of Jim Beam.

"Here, allow me," he said, fishing it out of the drawer. He gave the bottle to Rollins, who cracked it open and swallowed a long, long draught.

"Better?"

Rollins nodded.

"We were discussing Tampa and Bonita," Mac reminded him.

"Right," Rollins said, his throat still on fire, but at least he could talk again. "They're just contract labor, so we don't have any records on file. But somebody told me they live at a motel near the lake. It's a fisherman's hangout called The Bait And Tackle."

Mac nodded. "Thanks for your time," he said. He popped the cylinder of Rollins's weapon, let the bullets spill out on the floor then replaced it in the open drawer, sliding it smoothly shut.

"You should get a safety lock on that drawer," he said. "And another on your weapon. With all the kids about you never know what grubby little hands might be pawing in your desk."

Stormy was glaring at Rollins so full of fury that he was afraid she was going to come over the desk and attack him. But to Rollins' immense relief Mac took her calmly by the elbow and guided her out the door, stepping over the downed guards.

He watched them go, fingering his tender throat. One of the guards sat up. Rollins snorted in disgust. "Useless piece of shit," he said.

He picked up the phone and punched numbers. Someone answered. "Mr. Novarro? Okay, I understand that he's not available. But tell him that Mr. Rollins called from the clinic. And tell him that we've got a real bad problem. A problem that is way over our heads here.

"Tell him it's MacGregor."

Allan Cole

CHAPTER TWELVE

THE ONLY LIGHT burning at the Bait and Tackle Motel when Mac pulled into the lot was a yellow bug light above the manager's office. Frogs and crickets were out in force, filling the night with their noise. A few local dogs barked at the strange vehicle. Then somewhere far off a big bull gator bellowed for its mate and everything became very still - especially the dogs, who scrambled under a pickup truck. A country dog does not bark when there are gators on the prowl.

He shut off the engine and looked around. A few boat trailers were drawn up in the lot alongside their accompanying pickups - two Chevys and a short-bed Ford with rounded rear fenders and indented step-ups. The trailers were empty, and he presumed the boats were among the half-dozen he saw moored just off the little dock that protruded into the lake.

Stormy looked the scene over.

"Ever notice how Ford's been lookin' so much better'n Chevy these days?" she asked.

Mac grunted-she was nervous and wasn't really looking for an answer. He opened the door and got out. Stormy followed.

They looked like your average fishing-camp inhabitants. Mac wore one of the extra-large Hawaiian shirts he favored – this one was decorated with sharks and roses. His bare feet were shoved into a pair of well-worn deck shoes. Stormy wore tight levis that emphasized her skinny legs, leather sandals, and a sleeveless fisherman's vest that showed off her tats. Mac glanced down and saw one of a bare-breasted biker chick brandishing a bloody dagger. He wondered what the story was behind it, but didn't ask.

They went to the manager's office, where a small sign on the door read RING BELL. He found the bell and obeyed the sign. There was no reply or sign of movement within. He rang again. Still nothing. So he leaned on the bell and didn't let go.

After awhile he heard footsteps approaching and somebody said, "Hang on. Hang on. Jesus H. Christ with the bell."

He let up on the button. There were lock noises then the door came open, and a fat cracker in a dirty T-shirt and jockey shorts opened the door. Scratching his ass, he looked up at Mac. Before he could speak, Mac displayed several twenties, fanned out like a poker hand.

The manager gulped and quit scratching.

"Tampa and Bonita," Mac said.

The manager eyed the bills, licked his lips then pointed across the court.

"Unit 12B," he said.

Mac handed him the money. He counted the bills. "Any blood," he said without looking up, "you pay for the cleanup."

He slammed the door. Mac and Stormy turned and headed across the court.

"Maybe you should wait in the Jeep," Mac said.

Stormy snorted. "I busted in more doors durin' my gang-bangin' days," she said, "than the mother-humpin' DEA."

He nodded. She probably wasn't exaggerating.

"Fair enough."

He slipped a neat little .32 automatic from beneath his shark-and-roses shirt and handed it to her. Then he got out his big Glock, sighed and fingered the tender spot at his belt line. It was the main drawback to his dislike of holsters.

Stormy grinned. "I thought your pants were kind of draggin'."

He ran the slide back, chambering a round. "Here's to an armed society."

Stormy shrugged and got her own weapon ready. She wasn't much into political humor.

Allan Cole

As they neared the unit, Mac signaled, and they both slowed to a creep. There was the sound of a door opening somewhere behind them. Then of a baby crying. They glanced around in time to see the manager, now dressed, hastily exiting the office. Tailing him was a dumpy woman carrying a squalling baby, followed by four fat, dirty little kids. They all crowded into a battered Chevy pickup and sped away.

Mac grimaced. "Proverbial rats and all that," he said.

When they reached 12B, Stormy got on one side of the door, Mac the other. He leaned forward and gently tested the doorknob. To his surprise, it turned.

He pushed, very slowly, very cautiously, and the door swung open without restriction.

Mac heard a small metallic "ping," and his heart rapped against his chest.

"Bomb," he yelled, grabbing Stormy's arm and yanking her away.

They took off running, but there was no way they could outrun the laws of physics. An enormous explosion rocked the complex. Flame sheeted up and out. Glass and metal were catapulted across the courtyard like shrapnel.

The force of the blast caught them mid-stride. They were hurled to the ground like crash dummies in a factory test that had gone all wrong. Mac tried to shield Stormy with his body as debris rained on them. Something large thumped the ground beside him then hot sand and ashes seared exposed skin.

Finally, it stopped.

He flipped over onto his back. Fire raged through the motel, and half-naked guests staggered out in a panic. He turned to Stormy, but she was quite still. Gently, he shook her. She didn't move.

"Stormy?" he said, but then he saw the slender spear of window glass embedded in her back and he knew she wouldn't answer.

He heard footsteps coming toward him and voices calling "What happened, buddy?" and "What's going on?"

"For Christ's sake," he said, "somebody call 911."

At the edge of the camp – shielded from view by an overturned whaler - Bonita and Tampa observed the scene. Bonita was delighted at their handiwork.

"That's bonus number one," she said. "We'll have enough for that new RV before you know it."

Tampa shook his head, dissatisfied.

"I'm sorry, hon," he said. "Guess I'm a little out of practice. In the old days, I would've got 'em both."

"Don't be sorry, Sweetie… We'll get the other by and by."

"I sure hope so," Tampa said, "because that is one lucky asshole out there."

"No sweat," Bonita said. "It's my guess, hon, that he just used all his luck up."

Allan Cole

CHAPTER THIRTEEN

MAC PACED THE hospital corridor, pausing now and again to peer through the windows of the treatment room where the doctors and nurses were working on Stormy.

Down the hallway, the glass doors opened and some rescue personnel entered. Lt. Snow came in behind them. As she went by the ER room she glanced at the scene and shook her head.

"I could handle this shit better when I was a snot-nosed beat cop," she told Mac. "No imagination." She started to light a cigarette, saw the NO SMOKING sign and hesitated. "Fuck it," she said and lit up. She looked at her friend through a curl of smoke. "Still nothing on her grandkid…We rolled on Angelside, but the clinic's been closed down. The staff scattered."

He frowned. "That fast, huh?" he said. "Strange."

"You want to hear strange," Snow said, "you should have seen the reaction we got when we ran Rollins and some of the other administrators through the system."

"Like what?"

"Like a call from my boss, is what. Who got a call from Washington to tell us to knock it the hell off."

Mac considered. Then, "Spooks, you think?"

"You should know, Mac. Least, that's what I hear about you. Maybe it's all just a bunch of bullshit rumors, but the word around town is that you're an ex-spook yourself."

He half smiled. "No such thing as an ex-spook."

"That's what I hear too." She took another drag and expelled a long, thin cloud down the corridor.

Mac glanced at the ER window. The frantic activity had stopped. Nurses wheeled Stormy away through a rear door.

A doctor emerged, blood-spattered and tired. He did not look happy.

"What about it?" Mac asked.

The doctor sighed. "We'll have to wait and see."

"Thanks, Doc."

Mac turned to leave. Snow gave him a questioning look.

"Got to see a man about some insurance," he said.

The cop snorted. "This time of night?"

"My man's a real hustler... Twenty-four/seven all the way."

* * *

A hour later, he sat in the oak-paneled den of Jack Talbot, listening intently as Talbot talked on his phone. Talbot was middle-aged, and favored silk robes and loud pajamas. As he talked he was feeding two seltzer tables into a glass of water."

"...Same as always, Bill," he said into the phone. "I needed it yesterday three days ago."

He hung up, made a face at Mac and drank down the seltzer water. He shuddered and made a worse face than before. "Christ, I hate that shit."

He looked at the grainy white dregs in the glass. "So this is what you get with age and success - seltzer and tap water. Shit, when I was young and poor it was all brandy and Dexedrine."

"Pour some brandy, then," Mac said. "You're a big boy."

Talbot sighed. "Not so big after quadruple bypass surgery. "They cut your chest open with a saw, then stick your heart on a shelf while they fuck with you."

"That'll get your attention, all right."

"Oh, yeah," Talbot agreed, rubbing his chest.

Mac nodded at the phone. "I'm guessing that was Bill Propp?"

"Propp's a good man," Talbot said. "If anybody can chase down a connection between the Company and Angelside Clinic, it's good old Bill." He glanced at his watch. "Shouldn't take long. He knows a guy who knows a guy in Records."

Allan Cole

He paused, looked Mac over, then grinned at something he seemed to find amusing. "Last time I saw you we were hoisting sail over a big damned truck tire somewhere off the coast of Cuba. Then I passed out. When I came to I was in a hospital just outside Arlington." He leaned forward, fixing Mac with his weary eyes. "How the hell did that happen?"

"I'd rather not say. You'd just get all weepy about me saving your life."

Talbot shook the dregs in the seltzer glass. "Some life," he said.

The phone rang. He picked it up. Somebody spoke and he wrote things down. Then he asked, "When was that? Tomorrow night?" He underlined something on the pad. Then: "Thanks, Bill. Go back to sleep. God knows I intend to."

As he hung up he gave Mac an odd look. He ripped the paper from the pad and dropped it into a shredder by his desk, which immediately whirred into life, chewing it up.

"Jesus, Mac, I really shouldn't be talking to you about this.

"But you're going to, right?"

Talbot took a deep breath. Exhaled. Then he poured water in his glass and fed in a couple more seltzer tablets.

"Remember Novarro?" he asked. "Angel Novarro?"

Mac sat up straight. "Hell, yeah," he said. "Biggest butcher we ever graduated from interrogation school. Ran death squads in Honduras until the government changed. Last I heard he was taking the fall for all their sins—past, present and contemplated."

"That's the guy. The opposition called him 'The Dark Angel.' Dramatic, but accurate." He drank some of the seltzer and made a bad face. Put the glass down. "Anyway, rumors of his doing the noble thing and falling on his sword were vastly exaggerated."

"In other words, nobody's after him anymore," Mac said.

Talbot nodded. "And talk about small worlds getting smaller," he said. "As we speak, Novarro is some kind of a big shot right here in South Florida. Board of directors of half-a-dozen insurance companies…"

"Including yours?"

Talbot sighed. "Including mine." He rummaged in his desk and found an old crumpled pack of cigarettes with a few smokes left. He glared at it for a minute. "Novarro's also on the U.S. Trade Commission for bananas and other tropical fruit. And he's the CEO of one of the most promising security companies in the state."

Mac snorted. "Typical agency shit," he said. "The Company puts everybody into insurance, fruit or security when they retire."

Talbot grimaced and wiped the dregs from the glass with a finger. Ate the residue and shuddered.

"Don't forget sugar," he said. "He's also into sugar."

"Oh, shit. You got the sugar boys, you got everything."

Mac couldn't help but blow some steam. "But Novarro was just one of our clients. And a renegade one, at that. Christ, Florida's full of ex-dictators and strongmen. They all come here to spend their last days getting their skins used to the kind of heat they're going to face in the hereafter."

Talbot pulled out one of the cigarettes. He examined it, observing with a look of sadness that it was bent at an angle. An imperfect means of death.

"You're probably wondering why he's getting the treatment the Company usually reserves for chiefs of station and up?"

"That question sort of comes to mind."

Talbot straightened the cigarette, then fumbled in his desk and found some matches.

"Apparently, old Novarro had himself a bright idea we bought in to," he said. "An idea guaranteed to keep some of our harder-assed allies sweet. As you can imagine, after September Eleven some pretty ugly faces started to look damn good to the guys at Langley."

Mac nodded. Made sense.

Allan Cole

"The thing is," Talbot went on, "some of those ugly mugs are pissed off at us for dating other people before 9-11 and don't know if they want to let us come crawling back."

Nodding again, Mac said, "And Novarro's figured out how to mend their broken hearts."

Talbot shrugged then lit a match. "Regular handyman," he said. He fired up the cigarette then took a long, deep drag. He exhaled, seeming to savor the deadly weed. "Don't bother to ask for details. I'm not on the 'need to know' list and neither is our Bill."

"But it has something to do with Angelside Children's Clinic, right?"

Talbot took another drag. "Why don't you ask him yourself? Angel's the guest of honor at a charity polo match tomorrow night." He looked at the cigarette with a twist of amusement on his lips. "It's at the Royal Palm Polo Grounds," he said. "Dinner at the Boca Club first. Your old stomping grounds, right?"

"Right," Mac said.

Talbot looked at the seltzer glass then dumped the contents into a wastebasket. He gripped the cigarette between his lips and opened his desk. Fished out a bottle of brandy and poured himself a good slug.

"It has long been my opinion," he said, "that working for the Company is like fucking a porcupine. It's one hundred pricks against one."

Mac laughed appreciatively.

Talbot raised the glass in toast. "To open heart surgery." He drank the brandy down then shuddered. Took another hit on the cigarette. "Did I tell you that I saw God?"

"No, you didn't."

"Good," Talbot said. "If I ever do, I want your promise that you'll shoot me."

And he poured himself another drink.

CHAPTER FOURTEEN

MAC AIMED HIS Jeep south on A1A, heading for the Boca Country Club. On his left, the Atlantic glowed under the moonlight. On his right, the Inland Waterway, which meandered a thousand plus miles from the Florida Keys to Georgia, was dappled with lights from dozens of luxury yachts.

Boca Raton was a once-small town that was suffering growing pains. The growth was all upscale, with multi-million-dollar-per-unit condos popping up along its twin waterways. The population tended to be rich and middle-aged to elderly, but heavily favoring the Democratic Party – a place for wealthy liberals to retire.

One of the jewels in the crown of ultra-exclusive Palm Beach County, Boca had been ground zero in the infamous chad-counting presidential election of 2000. Even so, it remained a place of graceful homes and gated-condominium communities spread along the gumbo limbo tree-lined banks of a myriad broad canals that carried the tropical rains away to the sea. It was a place of amazing colors: trees and foliage alight with incredible blossoms; homes and buildings painted "Miami Vice" colors of pinks and blues and emerald greens.

It was also a town with more doctors per capita than just about any other city in the United States. And so it was that when Mac pulled off the highway into the winding tree-lined drive that led to the Boca Country Club, his mind was definitely not on the amenities of Boca Raton. He had a cell phone glued to his ear, and was hounding the hospital for some news of Stormy.

Mac slowed to let a dozen or so white egrets cross the road, then continued on to the guard shack. There was a uniformed hotel security guy on duty along with two rent-a-cops. The security was beefed up, no doubt, because of the all the big wigs invited to the soiree. The guard recognized Mac, gave him a thumbs up for a greeting, and waved him through.

It was a balmy Florida night and Mac had the top of his 1987 Y7 Jeep Wrangler rolled back and his tux shirt open at the neck, the black bow tie hanging to the side.

Relaxed as he appeared, his tones were worried as he spoke into the cellphone: "Yeah, Doc, it's Mac." He listened, face grim. "Shit," he said.

He listened some more. "But Stormy's gonna make it, right?" He frowned at the doctor's reply. "Yeah, I know you don't want to get my hopes up. Well, there's no danger of that, Doc... Okay... Call you later... Thanks."

Mac pocketed the phone as he neared the entrance of the resort, which sprawled across nearly 400 landscaped acres. On one side was a private beach with fences meant to keep out the riff-raff. In reality, it was fairly easy to sneak in – Mac had done it himself many times when he was a kid. A winding road led down a wooded hill to a large parking lot, serviced by electric trams, that was surrounded on three sides by tropical trees and flower beds. On the fourth side were the grassy banks of the Inland Sea. A private dock poked out from the shore, meant for the resort's excursion boats.

The main building of the Boca Club was an enormous pink edifice with palace-like turrets and battlements that made it look like it was right out of the pages of the Arabian Nights.

When asked about the resemblance, he always said, "No kidding, that's exactly what happened." Then he went on to explain that his great uncle, Addison Mizner, had copied the old colored engravings from a prized first edition of the Arabian Nights when he'd built the place back in the 1920's. People didn't always believe Mac, so he kept copies of the old books on hand to prove the point. The tales had been translated into English by Sir Richard Burton – not the actor, but the 19th Century explorer who discovered the source of the Nile. Burton's tales were X-rated to the extreme and illustrated with fabulously erotic drawings. Among those illustrations, however, were marvelous lithographs of exotic palaces and villas fit for the Sultans of old.

"My Great Uncle Mizner was a hustler of the first order," Mack liked to say. "Never had an original idea in his head that wasn't a con." Then he'd grin and add, "That's why we all honor his memory here in Florida, the land of the super con."

He pulled into the valet parking area and stopped. As a uniformed attendant hustled over, a low female voice said, "I've got this one, Hal."

A young Latina stepped out of the attendant's booth. Even in her uniform she was a sight to behold, with a figure and face like Angelina Jolie's.

"Nice to see you, Lupe." His bleak mood was suddenly lifted.

"You, too, Mac." She came over, moving with the graceful economy of someone who spends long days on her feet. "Spotted your name on the guest list and was looking out for you. Last minute thing?"

"Something like that." He started doing up his collar. "Is my mom here?"

"Boy, is she." Lupe grinned. "She's wearing an outfit that must've cost a king's ransom."

"That's no joke," Mac said. "Check out CNN and you'll probably find at least one king missing."

Lupe looked pointedly at the empty passenger seat. "Notice you're alone," she said. "Need some arm candy for the festivities?"

Mac grinned. "Can you get away?"

"Hey, flaking out is one of the few joys of small business ownership." She turned. "Toss me my bag, Hal."

"Sure, thing Ms. Martinez." He reached under the ticket stand for a gym bag and one-handed it to Lupe. She caught it and hopped in beside Mac.

"Head down the hill so I can find a place change," she said. "They don't like to see the help in the hotel unless we're carrying luggage."

Allan Cole

Mac pulled past the main entrance and turned into a long winding drive that emptied into the parking lot. Tall stanchions lit the place up, but there were deep shadows to be found on the edges where the brush and trees were thick. He spotted a suitable place under a stand of oaks near the dock, wheeled the Jeep around and backed in, leaving enough room between the trees and the rear of the Wrangler to create a makeshift changing area.

"You haven't stopped by since that little deal you helped me with," Lupe said.

"I've been pretty busy."

"Yeah, I know-busy fixing things. Isn't that how you put it? Fixing things?"

Leaving the engine running, Mac exited the Jeep and went around the passenger side to help Lupe out. Instead of taking advantage of Mac's ingenuity, she merely grabbed a beach blanket out of the back, turned around and started changing. Mac didn't look away, enjoying the sight of her under the moonlight.

And a fabulous, and erotically demure sight it proved to be as she pulled out some frilly, perfumed things from the gym bag, including a sexy little cocktail dress, and transformed herself into a Boca high society debutante, revealing flashes of tantalizing curves and gleaming flesh beneath the blanket.

As she changed, she said, "I don't know what I'd have done about those hard-asses muscling in on my business if you hadn't chased them away."

"It was a favor for your brother," Mac reminded her. "He did me a good turn once."

"Maybe so," Lupe protested, "but it left me feeling like…I don't know-a moocher." Finished dressing, she tossed the blanket into the backseat. "I was hoping you'd stop by so I could at least thank you."

She slipped on a pair of high heels, shook out her long hair and turned around, posing with a hand on one hip.

"Some arm candy," Mac said admiringly.

Lupe laughed, delighted at his reaction. She stepped close and gave him a quick kiss on the cheek.

Not too far away someone else had an altogether different reaction when Lupe kissed Mac. The beautiful Latina had just stepped into the crosshairs of a scoped rifle.

"Shit," Tampa said. "She's in the friggin' way."

Tampa and Bonita were hidden behind a stand of trees at the entrance to the lot. He studied the scene, the night scope painting Lupe's back an eerie green. "Wish I had a jacketed round," he said. "I could put it through both of them."

Lupe stepped aside, and he quickly centered the crosshairs on Mac. Then she turned in his direction, and apparently something caught her eye because she reacted, looking his way.

A reflection off the scope, Tampa guessed, and cursed the tall light stanchions bracketing the lot.

The girl said something, then reached into the Jeep and flipped on the big halogens. Magnified by the telescope, the glare was so blinding that Tampa was rocked back, butting his eye with the scope.

"Jesus Christ," he whined, rubbing his eye.

*　*　*

Some pervert is spying on us. Happens all the time around here, what with all the thong bikinis." Lupe laughed. "Of course, we didn't give them much to see, did we?" she said. "Just a little kiss."

"Yeah," Mac said, somewhat bedazzled by the kiss and the soft form that had briefly pressed against him. "Just a kiss."

He cut the Jeep's lights, then killed the engine. Meanwhile, Lupe got out her cell and called for Hal to send a tram.

*　*　*

Tampa and Bonita moved deeper into the prickly thicket as the tram purred down the hill to pick up their quarry. Tampa was still rubbing his eye.

"The bitch nearly blinded me," he whispered.

Bonita paid him no mind. She was watching the tram carrying Mac and Lupe to the hotel.

68

Allan Cole

"I wonder if the boss knows MacGregor's here?" she mused. "I mean, we're supposed to follow the guy…to look for a chance to finish the job …and we wind up at the Boca Club. Where the boss just happens to be."

"Screw the boss," Tampa groaned. "I'm hurtin'."

"We'll both be hurtin' a whole lot more, sweetie pie, if we don't start gettin' in front of this asshole pretty quick."

"Guy's lucky, that's what worries me," Tampa grumbled. "This is twice he got cut a skate."

CHAPTER FIFTEEN

THE BOCA COUNTRY CLUB was impressive enough during the day, with the sea rolling in on the private beach and the cabañas with the reserved chairs decorated with the wives of the rich men who vacationed there.

There was also a second club—divided by the inter-coastal waterway—where the rich guys put their mistresses. By day they lounged around the beach club and drank while their wives complained about being left alone at night. At night they lounged around the Intercoastal club and drank while their mistresses complained about being left alone during the day.

"For some reason the whole thing reminds me of Bat Masterson's last words," Mac told Lupe as they strolled down the wide hotel corridor, admiring an exhibit of Spanish paintings and sculpture.

"Bat Masterson had last words?" Lupe marveled. "He was an Old West gunman, wasn't he? My guess is that if he had any last words they'd be something like…'Arrgghh!'" She clutched her chest as if shot.

Mac laughed. "Actually, Masterson spent more time as a sportswriter than a gunman. Covered baseball, football and especially boxing. He was there for all the great matches."

"No kidding. Okay, I'm game. What were his last words?"

"Well, he'd just covered a fight," Mac said. "They figure it was about two a.m. when he got into the newspaper office and rolled some paper into his typewriter."

Lupe goggled. "Bat Masterson could type?"

"Sure could. And here's what he typed…"

"His last words?"

"The very last… They found him slumped over his typewriter in the morning. He'd just started his column before he died and he wrote: 'Take ice. The poor get it in the winter…And the rich get it in the summer…'"

She thought about that for a minute. "That's pretty much right on," she said. "It's sort of like petty larceny. You know, for a poor person, it's the only larceny she's ever gonna get charged with."

Mac decided he liked this woman a lot. "That's always been my thinking."

Lupe looked around at the Moorish fantasyland décor that was the interior of the Boca Club.

"Did your great uncle really build this place?"

"For better or worse," Mac replied, "Addison Mizner and his partner, Singer, practically created Palm Beach County. Which is where the chads fell short, a presidential election was stolen in Florida for the second time, and where we all now reside—the shame of the nation."

"Never mind the chads and the second stolen election," Lupe said, "I know all about Benjamin Harrison."

"You do?" Mac was impressed as hell.

"Sure, but you can tell me later if you really think you need to," she teased. "What I want to know about is this Singer guy. Do you mean Singer, as in the sewing machine Singer?"

Mac nodded. "His name was Paris Singer. And I may or may not be related to him as well. He was hell on wheels with some of the local girls who were ancestors of mine, so we'd have to run some DNA tests to be sure.

"The story goes like this. My great-uncle Addison thought he was suffering from a fatal disease, so he came to Boca to spend his dying days in the sun. It wasn't much back then. Just a clapboard hotel with a wide porch facing the beach and a swamp facing on the back, with some fancy grub brought in by boat for rich hypochondriacs."

"Your great-uncle was a hypochondriac?"

"Boy, was he. He was also a drunk and a dope addict— various opiates were the family pleasure then. But at that time—a little after the turn of the Twentieth Century—he'd decided his days were numbered. So, he came down here to die because he wanted to leave a tanned corpse. Which is where he met Paris Singer, who also thought he was dying. And they sat out on the porch of this hotel…"

Lupe nodded, indicating the hotel they were in. "This very hotel?"

"No," Mac said. "I think the site of the original hotel sits somewhere under one of the tennis courts.

They were approaching the dining area now, where the foyer was decorated with a fabulous ice sculpture of swans being pursued by a semi-naked hunter in a boat, spear poised for the first throw. A big banner over the entranceway read: PALM BEACH CHILDREN'S SOCIETY.

Mack continued his tale. "For awhile, my great-uncle and Singer commiserated, both being victims of imaginary fatal diseases and all. But then after awhile, when neither one died, they started to get bored. And then they started to dream about business and real estate. Being men who had been so close to death, they gave a great deal of credence to those dreams. Castles in the sky. Hotels at the beach. Since they were reading Richard Burton's Arabian Nights, that's how they imagined everything. And so that's how they made Boca Raton, just like it was part of one of Scheherazade's stories.

"There's more, but it starts to get into boring real estate success stories."

"My brother thinks you inherited half the town."

"Lot of people think that," Mac said. "Mostly because of the name and because my mom's got a pretty hefty trust fund – but that's from the Flagler side of her family, not the Mizner's. The fact is, Great-Uncle Addison lost his ass in the Depression. Sold this hotel for a song. My beach house was one of his creations - that's all I ever got out of it. And I had to pay off the back taxes at that."

He gestured at the ice swans and hunter. "I live by my wits, just like everybody else. I've got my house and I've got my old Jeep Wrangler which keeps me broke restoring it. I like it that way. As my great-uncle used to say: 'There's nothing so comfortable as a small bankroll. A big one is always in danger.'"

Allan Cole

Lupe laughed. As they entered the banquet room her down-to-earth chuckle drew the attention of a middle-aged woman of obvious breeding and good taste. Her face and figure were the work of expensive personal trainers and plastic surgeons, her clothing from the very best designers and her jewelry—which she kept to a minimum—could have purchased the loyalty of just about any current Florida politician, up to and including the governor.

In short, she was Mac's mother, Farah Mizner-MacGregor. She spotted him, and said in cultured tones that would only carry in his direction, "Mackie, darling. You came after all."

Farah swept over, her dress clinging just so, her jewelry sparkling a little but not too much, her perfume preceding her, but subtly so. She offered Mac her cheek.

"I couldn't stay away, Mother," he said, giving that cheek a quick peck.

"You always did dress up well," she said. "Just like your father. He had such style. But then, all the MacGregors were known for their style and looks. Florida royalty, you know. Never would have bred with him, otherwise. Got to keep the blood royal blue. If the Mizner's didn't disown us, the Flagler's certainly would."

It was then she noticed Lupe, and it was with undisguised enthusiasm.

"Speaking of breeding," she said, "are you the one who is going to be providing me with grandchildren, young lady?"

Lupe blushed beet red. "Well...I wasn't...I mean, we aren't..."

Mac jumped to the rescue. "Mother," he said, "this charming young lady is my date for the evening. Since it is our first date, the question of breeding hardly seems appropriate." He turned to Lupe. "Lupe, this is my mother, Farah Mizner-MacGregor... and, yes, she really is this blunt twenty-four hours a day." He turned back. "Mom, this is Lupe Martinez. She owns the valet parking company that services the club."

Farah's eyes narrowed. "Parking is it?"

Lupe nodded, not knowing what to expect. "Besides the club, I've got half a dozen contracts in the area," she said. "It's a good business."

"I imagine it is," Farah said. "And I'll bet there are quite a few cash transactions in your line. We really must have lunch sometime, Lupe, darling, so you can give me a few tips about circumventing those nasty tax people."

Lupe laughed. But before she could reply, Farah grasped the elbow of a distinguished-looking passerby.

"Judy" she exclaimed. "I was just about to send a search party out looking for you."

Congresswoman Judy Perkins was attractive, tall and delighted at the encounter. She and Farah exchanged elaborate greetings and air kisses - each careful not to muss the doo of the other.

Farah nudged Mac. "Look, Mackie," she said, displaying her distinguished friend. "It's Congresswoman Perkins. The one I've been telling you so much about."

Mac tried to look knowledgeable, but could only give a confused nod and extend a hand. The congresswoman swept it aside and kissed him on both cheeks, crushing her large bosom against him. Apparently, avoiding being mussed up didn't include good-looking male constituents.

"Mackie," she cried. "How fortuitous."

She pulled him closer. Mac tried—without great success—to keep his chest from being mashed against hers again.

"I'm really in a lot of trouble here, Mackie," she said. "And I wish you'd agree to rescue me. Be a darling and please say you'll do it."

"Of course, he'll do it, Judy," Farah said.

Mac started to panic. "Wait a minute… Do what?"

The congresswoman tipped her bare shoulders in a most elegant manner.

"Oh, nothing, Mackie dear," she said. "Nothing at all. It's just that the captain of my polo team suffered a most unfortunate accident yesterday. A broken ankle, or wrist,

Allan Cole

or…well, frankly, I forget what he broke. The point is, I want you to take his place tonight at the charity match."

Mac was taken aback. "You can't be serious?" he protested. "I haven't been on a horse for over a year. Much less played polo."

"Don't disappoint the congresswoman, Mackie," his mother said. "You know you simply adore doing favors for people."

But Judy wasn't paying any attention. Instead, she turned to a tall man who had his back to them and tapped him on the shoulder.

"Good news, Senor Novarro," she said. "I've just solved our little problem."

The man turned—it was Angel Novarro, looking almost civilized in his tuxedo.

Rep. Perkins indicated Mac.

"Meet Addison MacGregor," she said. "He's a champion polo player from way back." She said to Mac, "This is Senor Angel Novarro, our star benefactor. He's presenting a check well north of ten thousand dollars to help our poor little orphaned dears. He's also a fabulous polo player."

The two men eyed each other with barely concealed loathing.

Novarro nodded. "Mac," he said.

Equally as chilly, Mac replied, "Angel." He turned to Judy. "I'd be pleased to oppose Senor Novarro." To Novarro he added, "Unless you have any objections."

"None at all," Novarro replied in icy tones.

"I suggest we make the match more interesting," Mac said. "A ten-thousand-dollar wager—for the children, of course."

Novarro made a slight bow. "Of course." Then he smiled a thin smile. "After I win, my friend," he said, "we really ought to get together and discuss old times."

"Actually, I'm more interested in new times, Angel." Mac's eyes were steely blue. "What's all this sudden interest in disadvantaged children?"

"It's not so sudden," Novarro said. "As one ages, one becomes more sensitive to the sufferings of one's fellow human beings."

"But you're doing it in such a big way, Angel. And I understand you've also been involved with the Angelside Children's Clinic for quite some time."

"No longer," Novarro said. "I had a little disagreement with management and withdrew my support."

"Even so, they're still named after you, right?"

Novarro made an expansive gesture. "Sheer coincidence."

"One thing our former employers taught us, Angel," Mac said, "is that there's no such thing as a coincidence."

Mac's mother didn't like the frosty overtones of the encounter and tried to intervene.

"But surely this is a coincidence, Mackie," she said. "Your meeting Mr. Novarro like this."

Mac eyed Novarro. "What do you think, Angel?" he asked. "Is it a coincidence?"

Allan Cole

CHAPTER SIXTEEN

AT THE ROYAL PALM Polo Grounds the turf glowed a deep emerald green under the big night lights. Mac and Novarro faced each other across the ball. They'd changed into polo gear and were mounted on two fine Argentine-bred ponies, who champed for the action to begin. Spread out behind them were their respective teammates—three to a side.

Novarro snarled, "I say bullshit on your coincidence. I'm no fool."

Mac grinned. "Yeah, but you've got your suspicions, right?"

As they waited for the starting whistle, mallets poised to strike, the tension mounted in the stands. The charity event was the first night match of the season, and the benches were packed with the rich and famous and their hangers-on. The clubhouse windows framed an even fancier crowd, all dressed in their expensive sporty best and snacking on silver dishes of caviar and sipping champagne.

Word of the grudge match had spread like fire in the sugar cane fields, and everybody was discussing the situation, wondering at its cause and making up stories when nothing better came along to fill the void.

Farah and Lupe preferred a front row box in the stands and so were spared the gossip and the stares. Lupe looked worried, not knowing what to expect, but Farah was smiling, sipping champagne and chatting with a friend on her cellphone about how "dashing" her Mackie looked.

Then the whistle blew and both men slammed forward on their mounts. Instead of going for the ball, Novarro charged his horse straight at Mac. Mac had bare moments to pull his horse aside and miss a full-on collision.

But that trick was only Novarro's opening gambit. As he whipped past, he kicked out with his spurs and connected with Mac's leg. Blood gushed from the wound.

Mac's pony danced away, and Mac—in serious pain—leaned over and whacked the ball.

It sailed down the field and both sides thundered after it.

Lupe was horrified at Novarro's attack.

"The man's a cheat," she said.

Farah patted her knee. "Never fear, my dear Lupe," she said. "So is our Mackie."

Back on the field, Mac charged the goal line. Novarro saw his chance and spurred his horse forward to cut him off. As they met, he swung at Mac with his mallet, trying to smash him in the face. Mac parried the blow, but instead of striking back he pivoted to the side and his mallet hit the ball.

The crowd cheered as it sailed across the goal line, scoring the first point in the match.

Mac and Novarro lined up again. The instant the start whistle blew, Novarro came at him as if he were going hit him with the mallet. At the last possible second, he stole a trick from Mac's book and pivoted, whacking the ball down the field.

The two men, trailed by the others, raced after it. They dueled for the ball, leaning down almost to the turf as they moved in a strange, violent ballet. Then, at a crucial moment in the play, Novarro went after Mac's pony, trying to club the animal. Mac blocked the attack, but in doing so he left an opening.

Novarro took it, wheeling his pony about and sending the ball racing for the goal line. A split second later it sailed over the mark, and the crowd was cheering a tied score.

In the stands, Lupe threw up her hands in disgust.

"This is awful," she said. "How can they let him get away with that stuff?"

Farah was amused. "Polo is for the rich, my dear. It should come as no surprise to you that the rich are rarely chastised for their behavior."

78

Allan Cole

Lupe's temper started to boil over. "All I know," she said, "is that if I had a gun, I'd shoot him."

*   *   *

Across the field, in the parking lot, Tampa had his rifle braced on the roof of a Lexus and the night scope fixed on Mac. Bonita was beside him, watching the action through binoculars.

"Fuckin' beautiful shot, hon," Tampa said. "Call the RV dealer. We've got our bonus on the hoof. All I gotta do is squeeze the trigger and goodbye asshole."

Just as his finger took up the pressure, Bonita gripped his arm, stopping him.

"We can't do it, sweetie-pie," she said. "Not now."

Tampa frowned, easing back on the trigger. "Whaddya mean, we can't do it now?" he demanded. "I got that sumbitch dead in my sights."

Bonita sighed. "No way Mr. Novarro is gonna want us to shoot that guy right on the polo field," she said. "Not in the middle of a match."

"Why'n hell not? The boss's cheatin' like shit as it is. I'm just gonna help him a bit."

"Trust me, baby," Bonita said wearily. "We can't shoot the asshole just yet."

"You mean he's gonna friggin' luck out again?" Tampa complained.

"I'm afraid so, sweetie… We got no choice in the matter."

"God damn it to hell," Tampa fumed as he lowered the rifle. "Nobody, but friggin' nobody, gives a damn about the workin' man these days."

*   *   *

At the start of the second half Mac managed to pass the ball to one of his teammates, then hold Novarro off while his side scored. Novarro quickly countered, beating Mac to the jump when the starter whistle blew then lofting the ball up off the ground and into the scorer's chest. Mac's teammate came off the horse and hit the ground hard. The ball came to a stop next to his head.

Without hesitating, Novarro lashed out with his mallet—barely missing the fallen man—sending the ball slamming over the goal line to once again tie up the score.

By now the crowd was on its feet, cheering and shouting for blood. Lupe couldn't believe the reaction. It seemed more like a boxing match or, worse, pro wrestling, than a civilized polo competition.

She snorted. "This is the so-called sport of princes?"

"Well, you know how it is with royalty, dear," Farah said. "After all, some claim Jack The Ripper was actually Queen Victoria's grandson."

Mac and Novarro continued their duel, unchecked by the officials, with Novarro using every dirty move in the black book of polo. Both sides managed to score two goals each, putting the match in a four-four tie as the final minutes ticked away.

Then, with the clock running out, Novarro cracked what might have been the winning goal toward the line. But it hit a divot and took a hop over the grass clod, giving Mac the split second he needed to get his pony around the ball. Whack! went his mallet, and the ball sailed out into the middle of the field. Men scrambled for it, and there was a mad melee; then it squirted out from the pack, and Mac rode down on it, driving it toward his enemy's goal line.

Novarro saw him and charged in from the left, trying to cut him off. He was a heartbeat too slow-as he reached Mac's side, the ball was already rolling toward the goal line, which was only a few yards away.

But just as Mac's mallet gave the ball the coup de grace that put paid to the match, Novarro drove his animal into Mac's horse. At the same time he hooked the pony's leg with his mallet. Mac and his mount were sent tumbling over, the horse shrilling in fear.

Hooves flailed and Mac scrambled to get away. At the same time the crowd jumped to its feet to cheer the ball as it crossed the goal line and the clock ticked its final second and the end whistle blew.

Allan Cole

Finally, Mac managed to get his animal under control and on its feet again. He stroked the pony, whispering soothing things to calm it. Now the crowd's cheers were for the two of them when they realized what had happened and that man and horse were safe.

Novarro trotted over to Mac, who grinned up at him, mouth bloody.

"I've had my fill of you and your coincidences, MacGregor," he said. "Avoid them in the future, if you please. I won't like it. And I assure you our mutual friends won't like it, either."

Mac snorted. "Mutual friends," he said. "Well, call them all out, Angel. We'll have a fucking reunion party to end all reunion parties."

Novarro wheeled his horse around and trotted away.

Lupe came running up and gave Mac a hug of congratulations. He winced. She backed off, concerned.

Mac laughed. "Don't go away," he said. "Just don't squeeze so hard."

CHAPTER SEVENTEEN

MAC SAT AS STRAIGHT as he could on the overstuffed couch while Lupe wound an Ace bandage around his ribs. He tensed as she hooked it into place, then relaxed and let her pull his T-shirt down over the bandage. He gave a relieved sigh and leaned back into the cushions.

"Just a couple of cracked ribs," he said. "Not bad for having nearly half a ton of horseflesh roll over you."

He popped open a bottle of aspirin, shook out a few then washed them down with a snifter of brandy.

"Brandy and aspirin," Lupe said. "That was my father's favorite cure."

"Your father played polo?"

She shook her head. "Baseball... He was Castro's favorite shortstop, a real go-for-broke kind of a guy, you know? But as he grew older, he got hurt more often. He used to dose himself with brandy and aspirin so he could sleep."

"Did he ever play here in the States?"

"He got hurt too many times for that," Lupe replied. "Castro and the other big bosses abandoned him. He and my mother sailed an inner tube to Key West."

She patted her flat belly. "I was still in her tummy then. My mom said I kicked so hard it scared the sharks away." She laughed at the memory then turned serious. "My father parked cars at the stadium VIP lot," she said. "That was the only job a busted-up ballplayer could get. And then I sort of followed in his tire tracks and started my own business."

"Which is where I came in," Mac said.

She smiled. "Which is where you came in. How did you work that? I've always wondered."

"I reasoned with them. Simple as that."

"They didn't seem reasonable types... Except for brute force-type reasoning."

"I try to avoid violence whenever possible," Mac said. "It's better to use your head, see what favors you can call in. That sort of thing. The only time violence usually comes into it is if things have gone too far and are getting away from you too fast.

"In this case, when your brother called me it was early days yet. Plenty of time to think and help other people think."

"So, you didn't have to beat them up, or anything?" Lupe asked, sounding just a little disappointed. "They went away just because you said so?"

"There was a small altercation during my first visit with them," Mac admitted. "I offered to pay the guy's hospital bill, but his friends said it would be too much of an embarrassment and I should let it go."

"This is getting really interesting," Lupe said. "If you didn't use violence or threats of violence, I suppose you warned them that you'd get the law on them."

"Actually, I did them a favor."

Lupe gaped. "You did what?"

He shrugged. "It was the easiest way," he said. "Seemed that the main man of the group had parents who stretched their pension dollars with a vegetable and flower stall at weekend events around Boca."

Lupe nodded. "I know the kind you mean. One of those farmers' market deals."

"Exactly. Except, the guy's folks had made an enemy of somebody at city hall. Don't ask why and how-I sure as hell didn't. Long story short, their license was revoked. But, as it happens, the mayor is my cousin..."

Lupe started to laugh. "You mean you got the heat off them in return for getting the heat off me?"

"Yep."

"Why, that's almost...artistic," Lupe said admiringly. "It goes full circle. Plus, now they owe you a favor, right?"

"That's how it works," Mac said, pleased that she saw the symmetry of his arrangement.

Lupe frowned. "Did this favor business have something to do with that bastard, Novarro?"

"It's an insult to bastards to call him one," Mac replied. "But, yes... the visit to the Boca Club... the nasty stuff at the polo match... it had everything to do with... well... what I do."

"Tell me," Lupe insisted.

And when he hesitated, she gently pulled him close, his head nestled on her bosom, and he told her. About Stormy. About Stormy's missing granddaughter. And finally, about his suspicions regarding Novarro.

When he was done, he fell silent for a long, long time. Then Lupe heard his breathing quicken. He shifted uneasily,

Lupe thought it over. Then she noticed him shift as if he were hurting again.

She pushed him back on the cushion and found the brandy bottle.

"More?"

Mac reached for her. "I can think of a lot better sedative than that," he said.

Lupe gave that throaty laugh and let him fold her into his arms. He jumped a little as her body bumped his ribs. She pulled back.

"I'm sorry," she said.

"I can take it," Mac said, pulling her back, and she fit like she'd been nesting there for years.

The little cocktail dress and lacy underthings seemed to vanish from her body and they made love on the couch for a long time. Then they moved into the bedroom and started all over again, leaving her cocktail dress in a silken puddle by the couch and a trail of Mac's clothing on the floor.

* * *

Outside, six dark figures moved along the beach toward Mac's house. Among them were Tampa and Bonita, but they were in the middle of the group, not leading it.

That job had been taken by a fierce-looking man with an Uzi. His name was Rico.

"When we cased the place earlier," Tampa said, "it looked like you could get in from the sundeck. There's sliding glass doors that side. Looked like a piece of cake."

Allan Cole

He pointed to the stairs leading up to the deck. "Only thing is the stairs. They're kinda rickety, but they don't squeak none if you stay to the outside."

"Don't give a damn about no squeaky steps," Rico said. "Don't plan to give 'em time to figure it out."

Tampa shrugged. "Whatever," he said. Bonita poked him in the ribs, warning him to keep his cool.

Rico eyed him, as if waiting for some sort of protest, but when nothing more was said he turned and led the group to the stairs. He looked back at Tampa and Bonita.

"You two watch the back door," he said.

Tampa started to get pissed. "What the hell for?" he demanded. "You tryin' to cut us out of the kill bonus, Rico?"

Rico shrugged. "Senor Novarro don't want no more fuckups," he said.

Now it was Bonita's turn to bristle. "We're not the fuckups," she said. "This guy is a clever son of a bitch and Novarro should know it, seeing that he had his own ass kicked not long ago."

"Just do what you're told, okay?" Rico said.

Tampa and Bonita glared at him, but there was nothing they could do.

Rico fished a com unit from his pocket and keyed it. He whispered into it, "We're on the move."

There was a crackle from the speaker, and a voice replied from the front of the house. Rico nodded, satisfied his men were all in place. Then he pocketed the unit and led the others up to the deck.

Tampa snorted in disgust. Bonita gave him a sympathetic pat, and the two of them took up positions on either side of the deck.

"James Fuckin' Bond Bullshit," Tampa mumbled.

"I know, hon," Bonita soothed. "I know."

CHAPTER EIGHTEEN

ON THE SUNDECK, Rico used hand signals to send his men in different directions. Two slipped along either side of the house, another mounted the outside stairs that led to the rooftop deck.

Rico assigned himself to the sliding patio door that opened into the living room. He paused, listening. He could hear music playing faintly inside. He tested the door—gently putting pressure on the slide bar. No good. It was locked.

He peered inside, and saw the shadowy figures of Mac and Lupe making love in the bedroom. He watched for a few minutes, enjoying himself, then got out his tools and went to work on the lock. He was surprised at what a simple mechanism the guy had. This Mac guy was supposed to be some kind of a badass, but at his own home his locks were bullshit and he didn't have any kind of an alarm system – not even a dog.

Personally, Rico favored dogs. At his house he had a big damned pit bull he kept mean and hungry so he didn't give a shit about locks or alarm systems either. Guy busts into his house, he's got to deal with the dog first, then Rico. And if Rico wasn't home, what the fuck did he care happened to the dog? He had a deal with a dogfight guy out of Alabama. Animal got crippled a bit, Rico had a standing order for him and his friends. Bit-up dog made one helluva guard mutt, that's for sure.

And Rico had a guaranteed method of making a dog his for life. Like he told his girlfriends: "Put a bag over they head so they can't see shit. Then you beat the hell out of 'em with a hammer. Take the bag off and the damned dog'll love your ass forever 'cause you saved they's fuckin' life."

The reason he told this story to his girlfriends was that it had a dual purpose, and Rico was a man who believed in economy of thought, deed and motion.

He wriggled the little twisted piece of steel in the hole and the lock clicked open. He smiled, pleased with himself despite the simplicity of the lock, and reached to slide the door open.

Then he froze in pure, friggin' horror, because staring right at him with big beady red eyes was the biggest motherfuckin' spider in the whole motherfuckin' world.

* * *

Marvez peered cautiously through the bedroom window. Rico's numero uno bastardo felt his eyes grow to the size of coconut halves when he saw the naked couple making slow, dreamy love. His dick rose up like a cobra and what little IQ he possessed plunged to earthworm status as his eyes locked on the scene.

A beautiful stark naked woman was riding a man – whom he assumed was his quarry – like a cowgirl on a horse, her hips plunging and lifting, then plunging again. A joke he'd heard a couple of putas laughing over jumped into his head: "Save a horse, ride a cowboy."

Marvez became so engrossed watching the lovers that for a time he couldn't remember what he was supposed to do. What he was here for. Shoot, maybe he'd wait a little bit a let the guy get it off. Not a bad way to die, huh? Then, with a start, he got it together. Rico would skin him for belt leather if he didn't do his job. He pulled back his fist, which gripped a large flashlight.

He was about to smash the flashlight through the window when he heard the phone suddenly ring.

The naked ride ceased and he saw the guy reflexively try to sit up under the woman. The guy yelped in pain at the effort and fell back, groaning a "Dammit." Followed by a - "Jesus, that hurts."

Marvez couldn't help feel sorry for the guy. He heard the woman laugh at his plight, then gently eased herself off, showing Marvez an erotic vista that would make a Penthouse editor weep. For some reason she looked far away but, at the same time, very sharp and clear. Marvez pushed his face closer to see better.

Man, oh, man.

The guy groped for the phone, but he was still startlingly in must, which only made Rico's dick get harder. Poor guy. The man groped for the phone, but only succeeded in knocking it off the hook. Marvez heard a loud, "Fuck."

Marvez saw the woman grin at her lover's plight, then slide off the bed to get the phone. Marvez bit off a groan of delight as new feminine vistas presented themselves. It was gonna be a damn shame to kill her, but, Jesus Christ, the pricks said no fucking witnesses.

He continued to marvel at how clear her image was, like a classy porno picture under a magnifying glass. But far away—not in-your-face close. Marvez appreciated such subtleties -so he watched some more.

* * *

Lupe said, "MacGregor's residence." Someone spoke to her and she nodded, then said, "Just a minute." She handed the receiver to Mac, saying, "It's the doctor."

Mac's libido instantly fell to earth. "Sorry doc," he said into the phone. He listened, frowning, as if he couldn't believe what he was hearing. Suddenly he realized what he was being told and shot up in bed, ignoring the pain.

"How is she?"

Lupe saw a fabulous smile spread across his face. A rare kind of a smile of happiness and thankful relief that made her glad she was there to see it.

"That's fantastic, Doc… You're a miracle worker. I owe you big time." The doctor said something else. Mac laughed. "Yeah, Doc. You can put a favor from Addison MacGregor in your book instead of a bill. That's how thankful I am. Any time, any place-just call."

Hanging up, he turned to Lupe.

"Stormy's going to make it," he said. He looked up at the ceiling. "Thanks, God."

88

Allan Cole

He gave her a rueful look. "I don't even know if I believe in the son of a bitch, but in my line of work, it's best not to...take..."

They both heard a creaking sound at the bedroom window. Lupe started to turn toward the sound, but Mac caught her chin.

He leaned forward, as if to kiss her, but instead whispered, "Wait."

Lupe waited.

* * *

Peering through a gap in Lupe's midnight hair, Mac completed the thought...."... In my line of work, it's best not to take chances."

As he spoke, he eyes crept cautiously toward the bedroom window, where he'd caught the creaking sound and the faint blur of motion.

The reason he'd noticed it—other than years of experience being alert for such oddities—was the oval plastic magnifier he had slapped on his bedroom window. Similar magnifiers were scattered around the house—all fixed to key windows. Unless you were looking for them, they were unnoticeable from either side. There were other oddities spread through Mac's house. He disdained ordinary security systems, because he was an expert at such things and he'd never met a security system he couldn't beat. Why not assume intruders could do the same?

Then whatever had caught his attention at the window was gone. One thing was for certain, though, it sure as hell hadn't been his imagination. He gestured to Lupe: act normal. She nodded, cool as could be.

Mac started talking again in his regular voice, betraying nothing.

"All I have to do," he said, "is find Stormy's granddaughter and give this story a happy ending."

As he spoke he leaned down and reached under the bed. He came up with a sawed-off shotgun. He signaled to Lupe again—talk to me.

"Uh...What's...what's the little girl's, um, name?" she adlibbed.

Mac slowly, carefully, pumped a round into the chamber and slipped out of bed. He glanced at his shorts on the floor but stepped over them. No time for modesty.

"It's Leslie," he said. "A real sweetheart. Her mother—Stormy's daughter—was a crackhead. Stormy did everything she could to get her off the stuff, but her daughter eventually OD'd."

As he talked, he crept across the room. Lupe pulled on one of his T-shirts. At the window, the shadowy figure appeared again. When Mac saw it, he motioned for her to get down.

She sank to the floor, still keeping up her end of the conversation.

"The poor thing," she said. "Leslie's lucky to have somebody like her grandmother."

Mac moved toward the window, step by slow step.

"Yeah," he said, "she's got a lot of good qualities, old Stormy. You can see that...once you get past...the...tattoos."

He lunged at the window, smashing through the glass with the butt of the sawed-off. There was a shout of surprise from the intruder, cut off when Mac reached through the broken glass and hauled him into the room.

He dumped the guy face forward on the floor, shards of glass flying everywhere. He tried to come up, but Mac hit him in the back of the head with the wooden stock and he went down again.

Mac kicked the gun away, then flipped the intruder over and gave him a look at the business end of the shotgun.

"Who sent you?" he demanded.

The guy shook his head. Mac raised the gun again.

Just then, Lupe shouted, "Mac. Look out."

At the same time she scooped up a table lamp and hurled it a gunman who had suddenly appeared in the doorway. She threw it with such force the cord was no hindrance at all. The plug snapped free of the outlet, sailing behind the long cord like the balance bump on an animal's tail.

The lamp hit the guy square in the face. He stumbled, firing wildly as he clawed lamp and lampshade away. Mac

Allan Cole

let loose with the shotgun, and the gunman was smashed backward by the blast.

Mac racked another round into the chamber and rushed to Lupe. On the floor, the first guy scrabbled a pistol out of his boot. He came up to his knees and got off two shots in Mac's general direction, only to be cut down by a shotgun blast.

Then all hell really broke loose. A hail of automatic fire poured in from both the window and the doorway. Mac pressed Lupe flat on the floor. He fired through the window then spun and put a round through the open door. Outside the window someone screamed, and the firing from that side stopped, but the bullets kept coming through the bedroom door.

Mac heaved the dresser over and kicked it in front of the door. That shield only lasted a few seconds—machinegun fire ripped it into ragged splinters that shattered across the room, sticking into the walls like nails hurled by a hurricane. Even so, the temporary barrier gave him some badly needed time. He grabbed Lupe and hustled her into the closet.

Once inside, he pulled a duffel from the corner and shook out a box of shotgun shells. He reloaded then shoved a couple more boxes into Lupe's hands. She took them without question.

Out in the bedroom, the gunfire intensified. Bullets hammered through the closet door, ripping the clothes hanging there into rags. Ignoring the assault, Mac flopped on his back and aimed at the rear wall of the closet. He fired, ripping a huge hole in the plaster. He fired again, then again until a large, ragged opening appeared, framed by pellet-riddled two-by-fours.

"Through here," he told Lupe.

She crawled through the jagged hole. Mac followed, pulling the duffel after him. They emerged in his den. He guided Lupe to the desk and pointed to the crawl space beneath it.

"In there," he whispered.

She nodded and slipped into the wooden cave. Mac fished in the duffel and pulled out a bundle. He opened it, revealing a .45 automatic wrapped in a pair of old jeans. He rolled onto his back and pulled on the jeans. Then he checked the .45 to see if it was loaded.

He thumbed the hammer back and offered the gun to Lupe.

She frowned. "I've never fired one before," she said.

Mac shrugged. He placed the .45 in her hand. "Just point it and pull the trigger," he said. "Everything will take care of itself after that."

She licked dry lips and took a firm grip. "Okay," she said.

Mac started away, but she held on to his arm. He stopped to see what she wanted and she leaned forward and kissed him. He grinned then swiveled and crawled away.

Lupe ducked back under the desk, ready for anything.

Mac slipped into the kitchen, keeping flat against the wall. He edged over to a phone mounted near the doorway. He lifted it, checked, expecting a dead line. To his surprise, there was a dial tone. In the silence, it seemed unnaturally loud.

He pushed a button—beep! Again. Another—beep!

His finger moved to punch once more, finishing the 9-1-1, when a man's face appeared in the kitchen window. The image was made huge by the window magnifier and as the man's preternaturally large eyes turned to meet Mac's it was like looking at a movie close-up.

There was a visible reaction of surprise, then the pupils narrowed as a decision was made.

Forewarned by the reaction, Mac dodged to the side as the guy opened up, shattering the window with his automatic weapon. The chattering fire chewed across the wall and almost found him, but he dropped the phone just in time and let go with both barrels. Window, window frame, magnified plastic blob and the gunman vanished.

Mac grabbed the phone to try again, but the cord had been cut by the gunfire. He dropped it then froze as he sensed a presence. He looked around and saw motion in the other doorway. He scooped up the duffel and tossed it at the door.

92

Allan Cole

Immediately, another gunman burst into the room, firing blindly at the duffel bag. Mac cut him down, but the guy had barely hit the ground when still another man popped up behind him.

Mac pulled the trigger. The sawed-off clacked uselessly—it was empty.

He threw the shotgun at his attacker. The man's gun was knocked upward and bullets ripped into the ceiling. Plaster and pieces of lighting fixture rained down.

Mac dove across the room, piling into the gunman. The man's weapon went flying; but he was a pro, and instead of following his gun, he pulled a knife and slashed at Mac. They grappled, Mac trying to keep the blade away from him, but the knifeman was incredibly strong. Slowly, he backed Mac up again the sink. Then he forced the knife up and up until it was pressed against Mac's throat.

Mac suddenly released his hold, and at the same time he slid to the side. His attacker's knife hand plunged into the sink. Mac grabbed the wrist and shoved the hand—knife and all—into the garbage disposal and flipped the machine on. The man screamed as the garbage disposal started chewing.

Mac got behind the guy, jammed his knee into his spine, then put him out of his misery by jerking his head back and breaking his neck. He let the corpse fall, retrieved his shotgun and the duffel and found a box of shells. He started reloading as fast as he could.

* * *

Lupe heard footsteps approach. She shrank back in her cubbyhole, gripping the .45 with both hands.

Legs appeared before the desk. They stopped for a moment, and she heard someone breathing.

The legs moved on.

She took a chance and peered out, and watched a gunman go to the door of the den and open it. At the same time, she saw Mac backing toward the doorway, unaware of the danger.

The intruder raised his gun to fire, but she came up pulling the trigger, and boom! the man was smashed down.

Mac jolted around, saw the dead man on the floor, then Lupe. He went to her and put his arm around her shoulder.

Lupe looked at the man. She whispered, "Is he...?"

"Yeah."

They embraced, each taking and giving calmness and strength to the other.

Mac pointed upward. "To the roof," he said.

"Okay."

He released her, and the two of them slipped out of the den.

*   *   *

In the living room, Rico heard someone approaching and ducked behind the couch. He peered out and saw the guy and the woman exit the den. He tried to get a bead on them with his Uzi, but he was still freaked by the spider thing.

Clinging to the glass door, the spider was so big it had looked like one of those suckers on Discovery Channel that eat friggin' birds. But it had a red lightning slash on its belly, like one of those black widow things.

Deadly damned poisonous was the word.

Rico was no scientist to wonder how a black widow was crossed with a bird-eating spider. All spiders in general scared him shitless. The point being that a big son of a bitch was waiting for him when he tried to jimmy the lock. Then he couldn't do shit, except stare at the spider clinging to the glass and wonder what to do.

Then the shooting had started, the flashes of gunfire lighting up the house like one of those violent light shows at heavy metal concerts. Still, even when he saw his men going down, Rico was frozen with arachnophobia of the worst order.

He finally noticed that despite all the action, all the shooting, the spider hadn't moved. He looked closer— tentatively at first then more bravely as his nose neared the glass and the spider didn't move. Finally he realized the spider had suction cups on four of its eight legs.

Rubber ones.

The motherfucker was a fake.

Allan Cole

So, he blew it out with his Uzi, raking the door all the way up, then across, then down again. Sneering, he stepped across the splattered rubber body of the spider. He was going to wreck the remainder of it with another blast when he heard movement in the darkness.

Rico ducked down and watched his prey come out of the den and move down the hallway to a flight of stairs. The firing angle, especially in the dark, was lousy. Also, what if the guy had some more spiders? Real ones this time?

Rico didn't want to take that chance.

He waited a minute or two then followed.

*   *   *

Mac led Lupe up a winding flight of stairs. At the top he paused to look around. Nothing threatening presented itself.

He motioned her forward and soon they came upon another set of stairs. These were wrought iron and curved up to a trapdoor set in the ceiling. He moved slowly upward, Lupe following. At the top, he started to lift up the trapdoor, but then stopped.

He raised a finger to his lips to warn Lupe then pointed upward. Somebody was there. Very carefully, he raised the trapdoor a few inches. He pushed the barrel of the sawed-off through the opening and opened fire.

There was a scream as somebody was hit.

Mac threw back the trapdoor and fired blindly in first one direction, then another. There were more shouts and screams. Then silence.

He rolled out onto the rooftop sundeck, chambering another round and firing into a charging figure. The man was thrown violently to the side, and Mac reached back through the trapdoor and hauled Lupe onto the roof. He rose to his knees, peering around.

There was nothing to see except dead men.

He motioned for Lupe to follow and went to the outside staircase. Cautiously, he looked down into the driveway. Nothing in sight except, his unguarded Jeep. Then he remembered and slapped his jeans' pockets.

Shit, no keys.

He leaned close and whispered, "Can you hotwire a jeep?" It was Mac's educated guess that she'd grown up surrounded by backyard mechanics.

Lupe's wide grin told him he'd guessed right. She whispered back, "Two red, next to the ignition, right?"

Mac nodded and motioned her on with the shotgun. "Go."

She hurried to the Jeep while he played rear guard, eyes sweeping this way and that for signs of danger. She slid behind the wheel, popped the glovebox and rummaged inside, spilling stuff on the floor. Finally she came up with a pack of matches and a bottle opener, with an old beer cap stuck in its mouth. She displayed her find with a look of victory.

Mac frowned. What the hell?

Lupe just shrugged, and popped out the jagged-edged bottle cap. Then she fumbled under the dash and jerked out a tangle of wires. Quickly, she sorted through them. Found the two red wires, which she nipped with the sharp edge of the bottle cap, cutting through the sheath. She lit a match, melted the plastic and peeled the covering back, exposing bare wire.

"Okay, here we go," she whispered.

She twisted the wires together. There was a sputter, then the engine roared into life.

Mac started to hop into the passenger's side, but just then the garage door slammed open. A man jumped out. Mac swung the shotgun up, but it got hung up on the door.

Lupe didn't waste a second. She jammed her foot to the floor and the Jeep surged ahead. The man screamed and there was a burst of gunfire and then she rolled over the guy, crushing him. The Jeep careened forward, ramming the far wall. Boxes on overhead shelves spilled, burying the Jeep.

Mac rushed to Lupe's side, pulled the door open and hurled things aside to drag her out.

"We'll have to make a run for it," he said.

"Thought we might," she said.

They started out of the garage, moving quietly as they could, but just as they exited into the night air they heard

Allan Cole

something thump overhead. Mac looked up, his shotgun ready. He saw a man peering down from the roof, an Uzi aimed squarely at them.

The man grinned. "Where's your fuckin' spiders now, huh, asshole?" he said.

"What the hell are you talking about?" Mac said.

* * *

On the beach side, Tampa and Bonita were still at their posts on either side of the staircase. They heard chattering gunfire from the front. Tampa cocked his ear at the sound.

"That's an Uzi," he said. "Must be Rico."

Then there were a series of much slower, louder gunshots.

"A shotgun," he said. "Probably the asshole."

The firing intensified and became a full-out gun battle. Then it stopped, and there was dead silence.

"I think it's over," Tampa said. He frowned. "I wonder who won?"

The silence was broken by the single blast of a shotgun.

"The asshole got lucky again," Bonita said.

And the two whirled and ran like hell.

CHAPTER NINETEEN

NOVARRO WAS AT the wheel of the Humvee, fields whipping past him on one side, half-completed condominium complexes on the other.

"It's my own private curse," he told Hanson, who sat beside him smoking a thick Cuban cigar. "All my life I have been bedeviled by single-minded fools suffering from a misguided sense of justice."

Hanson politely turned his head and blew a cloud of smoke away from Novarro into the back, where their bodyguard sat, automatic weapon across his lap. The bodyguard was a hard-looking man, used to abuse, but the smoke was so bad he couldn't help but cough.

Hanson sneered at his weakness then turned back to Novarro.

"It's not all that bad, Mr. Novarro," he said. "I've seen worse. So have you. Shit, we had those Amnesty International creeps down in Belize who screwed with our interrogation business. Sent them packing, didn't we?"

Novarro smiled in appreciation of the memory.

"It was such a lovely business," he said. "Most countries have terrible interrogators. They are either too vicious or too kind. You have to know how to coax a man along—know his tolerance for pain and humiliation—to do a really good job of work."

"And that's what we gave them, all right," Hanson said. "Gave them a really good job of work. Without the expense of training and maintaining professional teams. Send them to us, with a list of what you want to know, and at a thousand dollars an hour we deliver it all up."

Novarro frowned. "We could have used the information we gleaned to make even more money," he said. "But the operation, alas, had to end well before it had achieved its business plateau."

"Amnesty International," Hanson said bitterly.

"We should do something about them by-and-by," Novarro said.

"Don't worry," Hanson replied. "The Company is of the same mind. Take care of 'em along with those Red Cross wimps who fucked with our methods in Iraq."

He puffed angrily on his cigar. "I mean, we were gettin' back into our own over there. Crackin' bones and stickin' rods up their asses until they talked. Then everybody got all limp-wristed on us and ran to Congress."

He snorted. "Amateurs. They'll get you every time. They don't realize that if you want a man to talk you gotta hurt him. Hurt him bad. Make him pay attention. Focus on the question you need answered."

Novarro was getting bored. He'd heard this from Hanson more times than he liked to recall. But he didn't like being impolite.

"Never mind them, my friend," he said. "Our problem is much worse than a group of limp-wristed liberals weeping and gnashing their teeth over so-called human rights."

"You mean MacGregor," Hanson said.

Novarro scowled. "Yes. MacGregor."

"What's the deal?" Hanson said, rolling his big shoulders. "He's just one guy."

Novarro snorted. "You don't know him," he said. "MacGregor's like that French detective in Les Miserables. A true Javert. Once he gets his teeth into you he never lets go."

"So what? We shuttered the clinic. Scattered the staff. All we have to do is deliver the goods and we're home free. We can start up again somewhere else and pretty soon we'll have enough money to buy half the world-and enough clout with the Agency to tell the other half to go fuck itself."

Despite the words of comfort, Novarro kept worrying the bone. "There are too many chances for complications," he said. "Ruinous complications. After all, there are fifty children…resting…in our boathouse. Originally, our plan was to slip them out in small groups. Put them on boats and deliver them to Honduras, where we could start auctioning the parts."

Hanson nodded-he could see where Novarro was going.

"Maybe we should just do it in one go… Get a bigger boat. Something fast. Really fast." He snapped his fingers as the idea came. "You want a fast ship?" he said. "I can deliver, no problem."

He paused and took another toke on his cigar. Breathed out smoke, letting it curl back along the roof. The bodyguard coughed again.

Then: "Don't mean to be rude, but I'll want a bigger percentage for my trouble, if you don't mind."

Novarro shrugged. "I don't mind at all," he said. "At this moment in time percentages are not my concern."

His cell phone rang, and he fished it out and answered it.

"Yes?" He listened a moment, eyes narrowing. "You are certain it is him?" He listened some more. Then: "Excellent. Stay with him. I'll meet up with you in a few minutes."

Novarro pocketed the phone and started to look for a place to turn the Humvee around. Hanson looked over at him, guessing what was happening.

"MacGregor?" he said.

"None other."

"Havin' it delivered, huh, amigo?" Hanson joked.

Novarro laughed, and with great pleasure Hanson blew thick, poisonous smoke rings that drifted back to envelope the long-suffering guard.

Allan Cole

CHAPTER TWENTY

MAC CRUISED ALONG the highway. They passed a sign that read: Lake Okeechobee—Ten Miles.

"Who's this mysterious person we're going to see?" Lupe asked.

"Albert Gomez," Mac said. "Everybody calls him Mad Albert." He chuckled. "It fits, believe me."

She raised an eyebrow. "Why are we going to see a crazy guy?" she asked. "Aren't things bad enough?"

"Albert's more eccentric than crazy," Mac said. "He's a biologist working the lake district for the university. World's greatest expert on frogs and frog diseases, I'm told. It's got to be true because, Jesus, he can go on about frogs for hours."

"But that's not why we're going to see him, right?"

Mac nodded. "He found something the other day that might bear on Leslie's whereabouts," he said. "Probably nothing to it. But it's worth a shot."

Lupe's brow furrowed. "Isn't Gomez one of your many middle names?"

He gave her a look, and she blushed.

"I wasn't snooping on you," she said. "My brother said you had some Latino blood. I wasn't all that hot on some strange gringo rushing in to save the day, is all."

"Perfectly understandable." Mac thought a minute, figuring out how to boil it down. Then he said, "The Gomezes were originally Portuguese. Descended from a famous pirate who escaped the British fleet and hid out in the swamps for years. The story is that he lived for one hundred and twenty years."

Lupe was amused. "And you believe that?"

"There's evidence," Mac replied. "Not irrefutable evidence, but enough to make a relative feel pretty good about having genes programmed for a long life."

"That's awfully good," Lupe said, "living one hundred and twenty years before old age catches up to you."

Mac chuckled. "Actually, it wasn't old age that got him in the end. At least, that's the story, anyway."

"You mean he didn't die of natural causes?"

"Not at all… Seems he went fishing in the swamp. The boat got stuck and when he tried to shove off his boot was caught in some roots. Boat went one way, he stayed with the roots and after a time he drowned."

"My God," Lupe said. "That's an amazing story."

"I read an old newspaper clipping about him," Mac said, "where Gomez told the interviewer the reason he'd lived so long was that God had forgotten him."

"That's a terrible, terrible thought," Lupe said.

"I guess you have a different opinion of God than I do," Mac said. He glanced over at Lupe. "As you've probably gathered from all this blather, Albert Gomez is one of my cousins."

Lupe couldn't help but laugh at this. "Actually, my guess is that just about everybody's your cousin, Mac."

"You're not," he said. "At least I hope you're not. And if you are, I pray that it's of the kissing cousins variety."

"We did more than kiss," she pointed out.

Mac chuckled. "I know."

Lupe gave that throaty laugh of hers then leaned over to kiss him. But then she jolted back, shouting: "Look out."

* * *

A pickup truck boomed up beside the Jeep, souped-up engine roaring like an Indy 500 car. Tampa was at the wheel, Bonita riding shotgun—literally. As they came up on Mac's side, she shoved a sawed-off out her window and aimed at him.

Mac jerked the wheel, and the shotgun blew out the Jeep's windshield. Tampa anticipated the maneuver- he crashed the pickup truck into the Jeep and held it there, body against body. Metal shredding. Sparks flying. Tires smoking.

Mac fought to keep the wheel under control. For just a flyspeck in time he agonized over the awful damage being done to his beautifully restored 1987 YJ Wrangler. Shit, shit, shit, he thought. Then he suddenly slammed on the brakes.

102

Allan Cole

The pickup kept going straight, but Mac did a bootleg turn and in half a heartbeat the Jeep was heading in the opposite direction. He only gained a little time by his maneuver-Tampa was no greenhorn in the game of car versus car. In an instant, he was turned around and roaring after them.

Bonita leaned out the window and fired. The back seat of the Jeep was ripped to shreds. Heavy pellets ripped up the dash. Lupe's seatbelt was shredded at the holder. G-forces threw her around, but she grabbed for the overhead rollbar and saved herself from being thrown out of the Jeep. Bonita fired again. Pellets whipped all around them, slashing cloth and metal. Miraculously, neither Lupe or Mac were hurt.

Tampa roared toward Mac's vehicle. He had two thick iron bars welded to his front end, making his pickup look like a charging bull. He slammed into the Jeep, driving it forward, the iron bars ripping out swaths of metal.

Mac fought like hell to keep control. Tampa came at him again, and this time the bars speared the rear gates. Tampa pressed the pedal to the metal, lifting the Jeep right off the ground. He raced onward, the Jeep's rear wheels spinning helplessly.

Mac reached under the dash and jerked out an NOS lever. New life surged into the engine as the nitrous oxide spurted from the canister and the front wheels dug in, pulling away. The Jeep jerked loose from the pickup's horns, slamming to the road and taking off. Then a rear tire blew and once again, he was fighting to keep the Jeep under control. This time he was out of tricks and room to maneuver.

Suddenly he was forced into the wrong lane. He saw a big semi up ahead barreling down on him, a load of tiles swaying back and forth. He tried to dodge it, but Tampa rammed him again. The steering wheel cracked around, nearly breaking Mac's wrist.

Tampa kept the pressure up then turned the front end into the Jeep. Lupe was jammed against Mac by the force of the collision, pinning him against the door.

Then the Jeep's wheels hit a low rail and flipped...once...twice...and then landed right-side-up in a freshly plowed field, its remaining tires bursting and its rims digging into the dirt.

Lupe was catapulted out of the Jeep. The grace of some higher being must have been with her, because she did slow somersault in the air and skated on her butt across soft dirt and came to halt, unhurt.

Mac stayed with the Jeep, instinctively killing the engine to keep a fire from igniting the spilled gas.

Tampa wheeled his pickup about and charged across the field. But Mac still had sense enough to roll out of the Jeep, drawing his gun. Acting on sheer instinct, he came up and got off two quick shots. Although both missed, they were close enough to force Tampa to take defensive action. He hit the brakes and slammed to a bone-wrenching stop.

Bonita leaned out to return fire, making Mac drop to the ground. Then she spotted Lupe about ten yards to the side, just getting to her feet, wobbly and dazed from shock.

Tampa saw her at the same time. "Get the bitch," he shouted.

Bonita piled out of the pickup. She sent a scattergun load at Mac, driving him down she raced to Lupe, reloading as she ran.

Lupe tried to resist, but Bonita put the shotgun against her head, using her for a shield as she backed toward the pickup. Mac tried to get a bead on her, but with Lupe in the way it was an impossible shot.

At the pickup, Bonita shoved Lupe inside, jumped in after her, and Tampa floored it, sending the pickup racing back toward the highway, spitting dirt in its wake. Mac sprinted after them, managed to get a hand on the tailgate...and was dragged for several feet. He tried to muscle himself up and over the side. Tampa jerked the wheel from side to side, breaking Mac's grip and slamming him to the earth.

Spitting dirt, Mac got to his feet, gun raised, looking for a shot, but the pickup truck was back on the highway,

104

Allan Cole

speeding around a curve. Mac spun and raced back to the Jeep. He forced the passenger side door open—torn metal squealing in protest—and pawed through the debris on the floor. He finally came up with his cell phone and snapped it open to call.

Before he could speed dial, the phone rang. He jumped as if stung. Then, cautiously, he answered.

"That was quite a show, MacGregor," Novarro said. "Quite a show."

*   *   *

Down the road, Novarro peered through the Humvee's window, grinning as Mac spun about, eyes wild. Next to him, Hanson laughed aloud at the sad figure standing by the wrecked Jeep.

"Here is how we are going to proceed, MacGregor," Novarro said. "I have something of yours that you seem to value. Do not interfere with my affairs, and when my business is concluded, you can have her back."

*   *   *

Mac sneered. "You expect me to believe that?" he snarled into the phone.

"You don't have a choice," Novarro said. "Trifle with me and I'll start sending your pretty little playmate back piece by piece. Do what I tell you, and she will at least have a chance of surviving."

Through clenched teeth, Mac said, "You're going to have me on your ass for the rest of your miserable life, Novarro."

Before he could say more, he heard the rumble of an engine and looked up to see Novarro's Humvee cruising by.

Novarro waved to him out the window, then gunned it and disappeared down the road.

Mac slammed his fist against the Jeep's hood in frustration. He started to call for help but just then, across the highway, he spotted a sign that towered over a stand of trees. It read: **BIG BILL'S BIG BIKES**

He pocketed the phone and raced toward the sign.

105

CHAPTER TWENTY-ONE

BIG BILL BENNETT sat on the porch of his double-wide trailer office munching his way through a box of jelly doughnuts, which he washed down with diet cola. He was nearly six and a half feet tall and weighed well over three hundred pounds, which he tried to cover with a super duper-size Miami Dolphins jersey, crammed with autographs of the team members.

A drop of jelly fell from his lips, nearly soiling the precious jersey, but he caught it on a finger with practiced ease and sucked it down. He started to take another doughnut, then hesitated. His wife had been bugging him about losing weight, as had his doctor. Then he thought, Screw 'em. You only live once, Billy Boy and he scooped up another jelly-filled cake.

Sighing contentedly, he lifted his eyes to gaze out on his beloved lot. Scores upon scores of freshly-washed bikes met his loving gaze. They were divided first by New and Used. And second, by maker: Harley, Honda, BMW – solid white folks transportation. Next, were your rice burners: Suzuki, Yamaha, Hyosung. Big Bill didn't like carrying those bikes, but, sadly, there were certain folks who preferred those Godless machines, and who was Big Bill to do something so sinfully un-American as to spurn their money?

It was a quiet day, one of a series of uncomfortably quiet days that had followed the latest hurricane season. Folks hadn't been out on highways and byways of Florida for a few weeks and Big Bill had sensibly laid off his sales force until real business returned. Meanwhile, he'd been personally beseeching the Lord Above to point some buyers toward his lot; buyers he was sworn to bless with his "Chains Of Life" pitch.

As if an answer to those prayers, he saw a man run onto his lot. For a second, he wondered if the guy had anything to do with the screeching tires and gunshots that he'd heard earlier. It was hunting season and you got a lot of drunken crackers running about this time of year. Nothing to get worked up about.

But then he saw the guy run up to a motorcycle – a made-in-by-God America Harley, bless him. A used one, to be sure, but Big Bill had a nice mark up on his used bikes, so no worry there.

To surprise, instead of checking the bike out, the guy only tipped it up straight and shook it. Seeming disappointed, he ran to another, shook it, then raced on, shaking bike after bike. It was like he was checking to see if there was gas in tanks. Shoot, Big Bill would gladly throw in a tank of gas to seal the deal.

He lumbered to his feet, painted a big smile on his face, and moseyed on over to the guy. He was a big fella – not as big as Bill, mind you, but he looked like solid muscle. He also had a worried expression on his face, a clear candidate, in Big Bill's mind, for his "Chains Of Life" spiel.

"I see you've got your heart set on breaking free of the heavy chains of life, my friend," he announced. "Well, I'm here to tell you that Big Bill is your kindred spirit, brother."

Usually, this got a guy's attention right off. But to Bill's surprise the man ignored him and kept jumping from bike to bike, checking for gas.

Puzzled though he was, Bill was still game. He followed the guy on his quest, motor-mouthing away.

"Yes, brother, it's the clarion call of the open road that you're hearing," he said. "The magic of motorcycling, I call it. Wind in your face, not a care in the world. And all with a low, low down and no payments for one full year."

He grinned at the guy expectantly. The no payments for a year always got them.

And joy to the world, it seemed as if the guy had finally what he wanted in a big Harley. Bless the man - sold American.

The guy pulled out his wallet. "I'll take this one," he said.

Big Bill's smile grew even larger. "An excellent choice, brother," he said. "Now, why don't we mosey on over to my office and discuss terms. In these difficult times it's not the price that's important, but the terms. That's…"

The rest trailed off when, lo and behold, the guy shoved a credit card into Big Bill's hand.

"Just bang my card for whatever it costs," the guy said.

Then he hopped on the bike, fired it up and roared away. Bill stared after him, mouth agape. He looked at the card, then back at the vanishing figure.

"…my motto," he said, finally completing his spiel.

*   *   *

Novarro glanced up at the rearview mirror and saw the big bike roaring toward him. He elbowed Hanson.

"MacGregor," he said.

Hanson turned in his seat and saw Mac. He pointed him out to the bodyguard.

"Shoot him."

The thug grinned, got a grip on his Uzi and crawled over the seat into the cargo area. Novarro hit a switch and the rear windows purred down. Steamy Florida air blasted into the vehicle and at the same time the bodyguard opened fire—a long chattering burst.

But it was a rough road they were on, making his aim unsteady. The bullets pinged off the tarmac all around the bike. Mac started weaving from side to side, and the bodyguard cursed as he ran out of ammo. Quickly, he dumped the clip and slammed another into place. He resumed fire.

One bullet glanced off the bike's handlebars, but that was as close as he got—all the other bullets went wide of their mark.

Suddenly, Mac accelerated, charging the Humvee. He came up alongside it; the bodyguard swiveled, trying to get a bead on him though the open window. Mac shot his hand out and grabbed him by the wrist. He jerked hard, braking at the

108

Allan Cole

same time, and the man screamed as he tumbled headfirst out the window and mushed face first onto the road.

Mac throttled forward. Hanson started to run down the passenger's side window, but before he got very far Mac powered up alongside the Humvee and gave the window a sharp shot with his elbow. The safety glass showered onto Hanson's lap. He cursed, shoving the shit off his lap.

"Get him, God damn it," Novarro ordered.

But while Hanson was occupied juggling his gun and sweeping away the glass, Mac stood up, and before Hanson could act, he jumped, sprawling on the roof of the Humvee. The bike hit the ground, spinning around and around, and then it was left behind.

Mac spread his feet wide and got a good grip on the roof edge with one hand. He yanked out his pistol and pushed the barrel against the surface. It was awkward but doable, and he started firing in a long stitching pattern all along the right side of his body.

Bullets slammed down inside the Humvee. Both men squirmed to the side, trying to get out of Mac's limited range.

"Can't you get rid of the son of a bitch?" Hanson growled.

Novarro sawed the wheel back and forth, making the Humvee sway violently across the road.

Mac had to grab at the gutter edge to keep from being dislodged and lost the gun. He clung there as the vehicle screeched all over the road. Novarro suddenly slammed on the brakes, and laughed aloud when Mac came off the roof, missing the hood entirely, while turning in a slow somersault as he arced toward the ground.

Then he gasped in surprise as Mac did a tuck and roll, coming to his feet in front of the vehicle then wheeling around, grabbing another gun from an ankle holster. He took dead aim at Novarro, who was momentarily frozen.

"For God's sake," Hanson shouted. "Move."

* * *

Novarro moved - goosing the gas. Bullets starred the windshield, and Mac had to dive out of the way of the big vehicle or die. He landed heavily at the side of the road, and the Humvee boomed away. He kept firing until the gun ran empty. He fumbled out another clip, but by the time he reloaded, the Humvee was far down the road.

He stared after it, panting. Then he turned and looked back down the road where the bike lay on its side, its back wheel still spinning.

Limping a little, he started walking toward it.

* * *

Mrs. Cortez looked up from her desk as the dorm room door banged open and Tampa shoved Lupe inside. Bonita stepped past him. The head nurse looked Lupe up and down with a critical eye.

"A little old, isn't she?"

"The boss wants you to hold on to her," Bonita said.

She nodded, then addressed Lupe. "Find an empty bed," she ordered, indicating the double row of drugged children. "I'll be by with a hypo in a minute."

Lupe's eyes blazed defiantly. "What are you going to do with me?" she demanded.

Mrs. Cortez shrugged. "There's lots of possibilities," she said. "We can sell you for parts-there's a waiting list for hearts and other internal organs. But if yours are substandard, we could always sell you to one of those live porn dot-coms in Belize." She smiled, enjoying the shocked look on Lupe's face. "I'm sure those parts work well enough, don't they, my dear."

Lupe suddenly looked like she was going to be ill. Tampa and Bonita roared with laughter at her discomfort.

Allan Cole

CHAPTER TWENTY-TWO

MAC NURSED THE battered bike along a dirt road that meandered toward Lake Okeechobee. The trail cut through a forest of old oaks and mangroves, draped with lacy Spanish moss. A few buzzards circled overhead, looking for opportunity. More than a few mosquitoes found theirs, settling on him whenever he slowed down, which was frequently.

It was hot, which did neither him nor the bike any good. Sweat stung his eyes and the many shallow cuts he'd suffered in his encounters with Novarro and his gang. His cracked ribs ached and his banged up knee was killing him. Moreover, his new motorcycle stuttered and coughed smoke, which burned the hell out of his eyes but didn't seem to bother the mosquitoes one bit.

The bike's drive chain was so loose it was practically flopping against the ground, but he didn't have time to stop and cinch it up. He just kept goosing the engine with a twist of his wrist and paddling his feet to get over difficult spots.

Then the dirt track spilled out into a large clearing, with a lean-to on one side that sheltered a pale-green pickup with badly scratched flanks and a dock on the other where a small, fairly new boat with an electric motor was tied up. Next to the dock, standing almost in the water, was a clapboard swamp house. It was perched on four sturdy stilts and had a rusted tin roof.

Smoke was pouring out of the open door when he pulled up, and as he cut the engine and booted the kickstand into place, a tall, skinny man with bottle-glass specs backed out the door. Armed with a fire extinguisher, the man was spraying a none-too-steady stream into the house, all the while jumping up and down, looking a bit like a goony bird, and shouting, "That's it, Marsha. I've taken all I can bear and I won't take any more. You're a whore for attention. The solitude-spoiling slut of the swamps."

Mac walked over to the house, listening to the crazy tirade.

"For two cents I'd skin you alive and sell your carcass as a hat to the next fisherman who ties up at the dock," the man cried.

Then a spear of flame shot out the door, and the man reacted in horror. A loud squawk could be heard from inside, and then a voice.

"Save me, Daddy! Save me!"

The man dropped the fire extinguisher and charged back into the house, crying, "Hold on, Marsha. Daddy's coming."

Mac leaned against the steps. Despite the mess he was in—and maybe a little because of it—he laughed. If there was a crazy edge to the laugh, there was no one around to remark on it.

Inside the house there commenced a great deal of banging, and then several pails of water splashed through the open windows. Finally, the man emerged, coughing and sputtering, with a large parrot perched on his shoulder.

The parrot squawked, "Save me, Daddy. Save me."

"Daddy's so sorry, Marsha. You have to learn to be more careful around the butane." Then he noticed Mac. He nodded politely. "Hello, Mac… You're just in time to help us muck out the house." He pointed inside. "We had a fire."

"So I noticed, Al," Mac said dryly. He mounted the stairs. "How's my pretty Marsha?" he said to the parrot.

The parrot squawked and flew over to perch on his shoulder.

"Save me, Mackie. Save me," she pleaded.

Mad Albert sighed. "She's such a slut," he said. He picked up a broom and tried to hand it to Mac. "Come on, cuz. Give us a hand."

Mac waved the broom away. "I'm in the middle of a fairly large shitter at the moment, Albert," he said. "I was hoping you could maybe help me out."

Mad Albert got excited at this news. "The shitter, huh?" he repeated. "What did you do, Mac? Something illegal?" He looked hopeful. "Are you on the lam?" He became more

Allan Cole

excited still. "Hey, I could hide you out. We've got plenty—" He broke off and looked at the house, then sighed. "Might be a little tight," he said. "And smell like smoke. But you know you're more than welcome, cuz."

"Thanks anyway," Mac said. "But that's not the kind of help I need."

Mad Albert scratched his head. "Okay," he said.

He popped open a cooler that sat on the deck and tossed Mac a beer. He got one for himself. Mac settled on the steps and drank deeply.

After he had cut half an inch of road grime, he said, "I want to ask you about the grave you found the other day."

Albert grew somber. "The little girl," he said flatly.

"Yeah, the little girl… Listen, Al, there's some stuff going on with kids. Bad stuff."

Al shook his head. "I've been hearing kids a lot, lately, Mac," he said. "Crying kids." He stared at his beer. Then, "Sound carries a long way in the swamps, you know."

"Yeah," Mac said.

"At first I thought it might be a new kind of frog," Mad Albert continued. "But it wasn't." He looked out across the clearing, a sad-eyed witness to man's folly. "Kids and frogs," he muttered. "Frogs and kids."

He paused and drank some beer, as if trying to wash a bad taste out of his mouth. He thought a minute then said, "Lots of 'em dying lately, you know. Is it the air? Is it the water? Is it us? Shit, before we find out— do the definitive study—they might all be dead." He grabbed Mac's sleeve. "Don't need any more studies, Mackie," he said. "Jesus Christ, it's as clear as the noses on their damned faces. Frogs and kids, Mac. Kids and frogs."

Mac gently untangled Albert's fingers. "About those crying sounds," he said. "Do you know where they were coming from? Can you show me?"

"Sure," Albert said. "But we'd better be careful. If it's the people I'm thinking about, they're a little scary."

Mac looked grim. "Sounds like the right place to me" he said.

CHAPTER TWENTY-THREE

A LARGE, SLEEK hovercraft cruised along the coast. It had full tanks and nearly empty cargo holds. On the bridge, standing before the com center, mike in hand, Captain Alfonso Mirasol was doing his best to fill those holds.

"Si, Señor Hanson," he said into the mike. "Everything is ready, just as you requested."

Mirasol was a seasoned seaman, who'd seen and done it all. At the wheel, listening to his conversation, was his first mate, Lt. Jorge Aru, a young man with too many illusions still remaining.

"That's not a problem, Señor," Mirasol said. "We can load the cargo tonight. Assuming that's convenient, of course."

Hanson's reply crackled through the speaker box.

"We're moving them out now, Captain Mirasol. Be with you in a few hours." There was a pause, then: "What about the crew?"

Aru glanced over at his captain, a worried expression on his face. Mirasol ignored the look.

"I assure you, Señor Hanson," he said, "that the crew was handpicked by me. Each man was promised a thousand dollars in advance and another thousand in Honduras."

"Good work, Captain," Hanson said. "I'll inform the boss and get back to you."

There was a "click" as he cut off. Mirasol replaced the mike and turned to Aru.

"Such easy work," he said. "I wish we could get a few more opportunities like this, my boy. We could retire for life."

Aru slouched at the wheel, trying to look experienced—nonchalant. "What are we carrying this time, Captain?" he asked. "Drugs or guns?"

Mirasol grimaced. "Children."

Aru started. He couldn't help his reaction.

"What do you mean, children?"

"Exactly that," Mirasol said, his tone overly casual. "Small ones. Niños. Fifty of them, to be precise."

Aru made the sign of the cross. "Mother of God," he said. "What is this world coming to?"

Mirasol shrugged. "Don't complain to God, Lieutenant," he said. "In this life one man's curse in another man's blessing."

*   *   *

Novarro and Hanson scooted up to the boathouse, the Humvee looking the worse for wear after their encounter with Mac. Bonita and Tampa waited for them in the doorway. They were both tired but tried to look brisk and efficient in front of the boss. When he got out, Novarro looked around the front of the boathouse and noted the absence of activity.

"What's holding things up?" he demanded. "The ship is ready for us."

Bonita tried to calm him down. "It's goin' kind of slow, Señor Novarro," she said. "The kids were all whacked out, remember? Mrs. Cortez had to shoot 'em full of wake-up juice and it's just starting to cut in."

Novarro frowned and hurried past them, Hanson close behind. Bonita and Tampa looked at each other. Tampa's face was starting to get red—Novarro's rude manner burned his butt. Bonita put a warning finger to her lips.

"Easy, honey pie," she whispered. "For me, please?"

He grunted something, which she took as acquiescence. She gave him a quick peck on the cheek, pressing against him just long enough to make him smile. Then they both went inside.

The interior of the boathouse was lit with spotlights that cast eerie shadows on the water, the speedboats bobbing in their slips and the long line of children moving slowly down the stairs. Novarro ignored the kids for the moment and turned to watch the men who were putting gas into the boats.

"Is there enough spare fuel aboard all these boats?" he asked Hanson. "They have to go to sea, after all. And we weren't planning on that."

Hanson fished out his cell phone. "I'll check," he said, then hit the speed dial.

Novarro snorted in disgust. "Mother of Mercy. Do I have to think of everything?"

At the top of the stairs, Lupe was moving through the kids, keeping low to draw as little attention as possible.

"Anyone here named Leslie?" she whispered to the kids. Whenever she saw a girl about the right age, she asked, "Are you Leslie, honey?"

None of the kids replied with more than a negative shake of the head. She was starting to lose hope when, finally, one of children reacted when she heard the name. She stepped out of line, turning her face toward Lupe.

"Here I am," she said in a small, frightened voice. "I'm Leslie."

Lupe got to her in a hurry. "I'm Lupe, honey," she said. "Stormy sent me."

Leslie's eyes glistened with tears and hope. "Are you here to take me home?" she asked.

Lupe bent down and kissed her. "I'll certainly do my best, honey," she said. "But we're going to have to be real sneaky about it. Do you understand what I'm saying? Very, very sneaky."

Leslie nodded. "This is like an Uncle Mac deal, right?"

Lupe laughed and gave her a hug. "Exactly, sweetheart," she said. "Exactly."

*   *   *

Mac and Mad Albert purred along the edge of the lake in the little electric boat. Mac was in the stern, watching for snags in the shallow water. Al was at the tiller, Marsha perched quietly on his shoulder.

It was getting late, and the sun's glare on the water made it hard to see. Al shaded his eyes then nodded and pointed off in the distance.

Allan Cole

"There's an old boathouse about three miles south of here," he said. "A new owner bought it not long ago. A real horse's ass, too."

"That's the problem with this world," Mac said. "We've got a lot fewer horses than horses' asses."

"Isn't that the truth," Albert agreed. "Except, well, in the old days when we had a lot more horses asses than we do now the horse shit got so bad in the cities that…well, I don't know which is worse, animal methane or burned gasoline. You know—horse farts or car farts."

Mac didn't say anything, fearing that if he did Albert would take it as a sign to motor mouth on.

After a long silence, Albert gave up and sighed. He said, "New owner's got guards all over the place. They ran me off once. I told them about my frog survey, but they didn't much give a shit."

"Atrocity-committing Huns," Mac said.

"You got that right," Albert said. "Anyway, at first I figured it was a meth lab or something. Except I didn't smell any meth cooking."

Mac thought a moment then asked, "Can you get me in for a closer look?"

Mad Albert nodded. "Hope we don't find something bad there."

"If we don't," Mac said, "I'll be so deep in the shitter I'll never get out."

Albert just sighed.

CHAPTER TWENTY-FOUR

THE DAY WAS WINDING down, and in the harsh glare of
the spotlights, Novarro's men hustled children aboard the
speedboats. Bonita and Tampa were in charge of this part of
the operation, pushing kids toward each boat until it was full
then directing the others to the next boat in line. The kids
were too drugged to protest the rough handling, although a
few whimpered and several of the smaller children were
weeping.

Bonita picked up a weeper and handed the kid to one of
the men on the boat.

"Put him in the back," she ordered. "That way the crying
won't spread as much."

Tampa gave her hip a squeeze. "You sure are good with
kids, hon," he said.

But soon as he said it he started to look worried—
frowning and biting his lower lip.

"No big deal," Bonita said, not noting his change in
mood. "I was one once myself."

Behind them, Lupe held Leslie back, letting the others
go ahead. She was trying to slow their progress as much as
possible. Her ploy worked, because just as it became their
turn to board the boat Bonita stepped in front of them,
barring the way.

"That's enough," she said. "Next boat."

At her signal, the crowded craft sped away, big engines
thundering with unleashed power. Some of the kids cried out
at the sound.

Tampa indicated one of the other empty boats. "Get
movin'," he shouted.

And the next in line rumbled up to the dock. Lupe used
the confusion of crying kids and noisy engines to pull Leslie
back into the crowd. She didn't really have a plan. She just

wanted to delay things as long as possible and pray to God that Mac showed up with the cavalry.

* * *

The electric boat cruised quietly through the reeds. Albert made whisker motions at his lips as he steered the shallow-bottomed craft around two dark shapes moving along the banks.

"Manatee and her calf," he whispered.

Mac nodded, and although he'd seen such things countless times, he still looked with interest at the mother and child lifting their whiskered muzzles out of the water to quietly munch the grass. The mother had a huge, ugly scar running down her back- the gentle creatures were easy victims of hotrodders violating boat speed laws, cutting up the slow manatees with their propellers. He saw Albert grimace and knuckle away a tear. His cousin was always deeply affected by such things.

Marsha, on the other hand, paid the creatures no mind. She was too busy grooming herself, fussing with Albert's wiry hair every now and then so he wouldn't feel left out.

Up ahead there was a sudden flash of light. Although it was still daylight, the swamp, with its tall moss-draped trees and thick underbrush, was always cast in deep shadows this time of day. Mac signaled Albert, who spotted the light, then nodded and cut the motor.

Mac slid into the water and swam slowly toward the source of the flash.

* * *

Woody Carlton was one pissed off cracker. He and that shit for brains, Jimmy Lee Walker, had been patrolling the path that ran down from the boathouse to the swamp for most of the day without one damn beer break. Fuckin' greaser boss had a heart the size of a gnat's dick, as far as he could tell. There was no god damned reason to patrol this area – what's gonna sneak up on you from the swamp, for God's sake? A gator, maybe, but that was it. But no, Mr. Greaser Novarro says patrol, so you've got to patrol 'cause the boss won't listen to no common sense.

And here he was, weighed down by a ton of useless gear and heavy weapons, sweatin' and gruntin' like four guys stuck in a two-hole outhouse, swattin' mosquitoes big as razor backs.

"I'm tellin' ya, I heard somethin' clear as day," Jimmy Lee said, leading the way down the path.

Woody snorted. Jimmy Lee was such a candy ass. Pissed his pants when he heard a twig snap. Then, just down the trail, Woody heard a big bullfrog croak to its mate.

"For fuck's sake, Jimmy Lee," he complained, "it's just some frog lookin' to get laid."

"By God, I know'd I heard somethin' besides a damn frog messin' around out here," Jimmy Lee insisted.

Woody sneered. "Bullshit," he said. "You always were a nervous sort. Pop 'em off at the sight of your own shadow."

"Bullshit, yourself," Jimmy Lee retorted.

Just then Woody saw something move behind a thick stand of swamp grass. Jimmy Lee spotted it too and gave his companion a victorious grin.

"I knew it," he said, leading the way to the spot. "Take a look at this," he said.

He parted a clump of bushes to reveal this crazy looking guy sitting in a boat with a parrot on his shoulder. The parrot made noises like a frog: "Ribb-itt! Squawk! Ribb-itt!"

"Boy, am I glad to see you guys," the man said, grinning like a mad scientist. "I found the damnedest frog." He indicated parrot. "Scientific miracle if I ever saw one."

Woody was totally disgusted. He'd hear about this from Jimmy Lee from now until Hell grew icicles. He lifted his weapon, aiming at the parrot.

"I hate frogs," he said.

As his finger tightened on the trigger, there was an explosion of water behind him. A strong hand jerked him back by the hair. A knee jammed into his spine and the pain was so fierce he was practically paralyzed.

Helpless, he watched the guy in the boat hurl the parrot at Jimmy Lee and the damned bird went right for his partner's eyes. At the same time the crazy guy bounded out

Allan Cole

of the boat and knocked Jimmy Lee flat with a bailing bucket.

Then an enormous fist slammed into the back of Woody's head and he hit the muddy ground face first. Dazed, he could do nothing as first he and then Jimmy Lee were immobilized with duct tape.

Someone flipped him over and he found himself staring up at a large man with a face as hard as his muscles. The guy stripped him and Jimmy Lee of their weapons, ammo and flashlights.

He offered the crazy guy one of the guns. "You always were a fair shot, if I recall, cuz," he heard the man say.

The crazy guy snorted. "Fair shot," he said. "You know very well I can shoot the sexual organs off a tree-dwelling rodent at a hundred yards."

"That's a terrible thing to do to a squirrel, Al," the big man replied. He gestured down the trail. "Okay, let's go see what these boys were guarding."

"Wait a sec," the crazy guy said. Digging into a pocket, he approached Woody and Jimmy Lee. Producing what appeared to be a vial, he knelt beside Woody.

"You really pissed me off, man," he said, "talking about frogs like that... Then you nearly shot Marsha."

Apparently Marsha was the parrot perched on this guy, Al's, shoulder. The bird's eyes were fierce as she stared down at Woody.

Then the guy uncorked the vial and Woody smelled something really awful. The man started sprinkling the smelly stuff over Woody, then Jimmy Lee. Bound and gagged as they were, they could only struggle weakly and try to squirm away.

"This is about two ounces of female frog pheromones," the guy went on.

Woody grunted, not knowing what he was talking about, but it sounded awful.

The crazy guy nodded in sympathy. "So many new things in the world," he said, "gets hard to keep up. For a man to know. So I don't blame you for not knowing. I only blame you for not giving a shit." He kept sprinkling the stuff as he talked. "Maybe my potion—Frog Potion Number Nine, I call it—will help you give a shit. Long story short," he added, "this stuff's like Viagra. But for bullfrogs. Soon as they smell it, those bullfrogs want to fuck. They think a sweet honey of a girl frog is pining for them to come and mount them."

He finished sprinkling, capped the vial and stuck it back in his pocket. Woody's heart was racing a mile a minute. He heard muffled squeal from Jimmy Lee – a squeal like a girl's - but he was in no position in criticize because he was squealin' too.

The crazy guy smiled in apparent satisfaction. Jesus, what a fuckin' monster, Woody thought.

"You're getting it," the guy said. "In about two minutes every bullfrog in the swamp will be right here trying to figure out where all the lady frogs are. And when they can't find them… well, boys, hope you can handle frog dick."

Woody groaned and struggled to get free. But it was no use.

Off in the swamp Woody heard the distinct sound of a big damned frog. "Rib-bitt! Rib-bitt!" Shit, it was so loud that it had to be the damned granddaddy of all frogs.

He looked over at Jimmy Lee. His partner's eyes were wild with fear. He was sure his looked no better.

Then once again he heard the telltale "Rib-bitt. Rib-bitt." More frog sounds joined the first. Then more still. Woody tried to cry out but the sound was muffled by the gag.

Then, to his horror, first one frog hopped onto to the scene. Then another. And another. They hopped forward, making that awful sound – "Rib-bitt! Rib-bitt!"

It was then that old Woody pissed his pants.

*   *   *

Mac and Albert paused to listen to the thrashing and frog noises behind them.

"Frogs can't really hurt them, can they, Albert?"

"No, no," Albert said. "They won't even get warts. Matter of fact, the frogs will probably keep the mosquitoes off of them."

Allan Cole

"It was still a pretty cruel thing to do, cuz."

Albert giggled. "Wasn't it, though?"

They continued moving down the winding path and soon they heard voices ahead as well as the throbbing sound of powerful marine engines. Finally, light glimmered from beyond the brush screen. Mac and Albert dropped to their knees and crawled forward. When the voices sounded close, Mac called a halt. Then he leaned cautiously forward and parted the foliage.

Through the gap he saw Novarro's Humvee parked outside the boathouse, but Novarro and Hanson were nowhere in sight. Several beefy guards patrolled the grounds, while through the boathouse's open doors he could see men rushing about.

Suddenly, a speedboat full of wailing children burst from the boathouse and headed out into the lake. He pulled back, shaken by the sight.

"Jesus, God, Mac," Albert said. "We've got to do something. Those are just kids."

Mac was only half listening, because he had just spotted Lupe and Leslie being herded toward the last vessel in the children's convoy. The man and woman doing the herding were the same people in truck that had grabbed her. He guessed they were the Tampa and Bonita he and Stormy had tracked to the motel.

He watched as Tampa fired the engine and the boat charged out into the lake.

Quickly, Mac checked his weapons and ammo.

"Lupe found Leslie," he said. "That'll make this whole thing go a helluva lot easier."

Mad Albert looked at him, impressed. "Got a plan already, huh? That's fabulous. Really fabulous." He paused to check his own weapon then said, "What do we do next."

Mac shrugged. "Same as I always do," he said. "Play it by ear."

CHAPTER TWENTY-FIVE

NOVARRO PACED THE dock, cell phone against his ear, the supercilious smile of a guy talking to somebody important on his face. All the kids had been hauled off, and two speedboats sat beside the dock. Hanson was at the wheel of one. The other carried two gunmen, Jose and Geraldo, who were lolling on the deck smoking and waiting for orders.

"...And you can tell the general he has my personal guarantee that the liver will be from a donor who is less than twelve years old," Novarro said. "So it'll be extra-strong. And virgin-it's never been contaminated by alcohol or drugs, or even tobacco. And the asking price is only five hundred thousand dollars."

He listened patiently as the guy on the line responded. "Yes, it is quite a bargain, my friend. Especially for a great man like the general. A man with so much gusto. So much to live for." He listened some more, his smile growing. "Good, it's settled then," he said. "I'll see you in Honduras."

He snapped the cell phone shut and pocketed it. Then he turned to Jose and Geraldo.

"Stay close," he ordered. "I don't want any surprises."

"Si, Señor Novarro," Jose said, bobbing his head meekly.

Novarro dropped into Hanson's boat and they roared off at high speed.

The other boat, however, didn't immediately follow. Jose cranked the starter, but the engine wouldn't fire. It only sputtered and coughed.

"Puta!" he yelled, swatting the engine.

A shadow fell across him, and he jolted in surprise. He looked up to see this crazy gringo staring down at him, streaming muddy lake water. As Jose stared, a large parrot flew down and landed on the gringo's shoulder.

"Looking for something?" the gringo asked, grinning a crazy smile. He held a boat engine's rotor cap in his hand.

The parrot squawked, "Mayday! Mayday!"

* * *

As the gunnies gaped at Albert and Marsha, behind them, Mac exploded out of the water. He was armed with a heavy pee-vee pole, which he swung, knocking both men into the water. Then he dropped the pole and dived over the boat to close with them.

The boat operator was the first to recover. He attacked with a fury, sweeping a boat hook off the dock. He lashed out at Mac, who leaned back, letting the boat hook swing through. Then he grabbed the guy's arm and bent it back, trying to break it.

But the man was no wimp. He was strong as hell, with a body and limbs like a defensive linebacker. He jerked his arm forward, pulling Mac half out of the water. Then he pivoted and slammed him back against the dock. He drew a knife, but Mac caught his hand. They grappled, the fight going first one way, then the other.

Over the man's shoulder, Mac saw that the other gunman had recovered. Standing in the shallow water, he leaned over the boat and picked up his weapon. He turned, ratcheting back the bolt to blow Mac to pieces.

He forced his attacker around-using him as a shield. But the guy evidently didn't give a shit. He raised his gun.

Mac spotted Albert coming up behind the guy. He had his pistol out, but he was hesitating. Shoot him, damn it! Mac thought. This was no time to be squeamish.

Suddenly, Albert reversed the gun and whacked the guy over the head, knocking him senseless.

At the same time, Mac managed to get free of the muscle-bound guy's grip. He jammed three stiffened fingers into the man's throat, knocking him back gasping for breath. Then he swung, connected with the man's jaw, and dropped him.

Anticipating what was about to happen next, he pulled himself aboard the boat and scrambled for the com unit.

* * *

Out on the lake, Novarro stared back at the landing, looking for the lights of the other speedboat. He saw the craft still bobbing at the dock, and he grabbed the mike off the radio unit.

"I told those two to stay close," he growled to Hanson, who only shrugged and kept his hands on the wheel and eyes on the course they'd set.

*   *   *

Mad Albert fiddled with the engine, replacing the distributor cap as quickly as he could. Mac was at the helm, hand resting on the mike.

The radio blared into life, and Novarro's voice barked, "What's happening with you? What's the delay?"

Mack picked up the mike, cleared his throat then keyed in. "Uno momento, Señor," he said, making his voice harsh and trying to sound like a Latino. "Poco problemo."

At that moment, Albert made the connection and slammed the hatch cover closed. Mac hit the starter and the engine roared into life. He aimed the mike at the engine compartment so Novarro could hear.

Then he said, "You see, Señor? She is fixed." He replaced the mike and turned to Albert. "You'd better get the cavalry in motion... Speak to Lieutenant Snow. Nobody else. Got it?"

"Sure... Lieutenant Snow." Albert climbed back on the dock, Marsha perched on his shoulder. "This is like some spooky Stephen King book about weirdo telemarketers," he said. "Novarro was selling children's organs on the phone... And you say the government—our government—is backing him?"

Mac sighed. "Don't think on it too hard, Albert," he said. "It'll drive you crazier than you already are."

He tossed off the ropes, gunned the engine and sped away. Albert stared after him. Marsha squawked, "Save me, Daddy! Save me!"

126

Allan Cole

CHAPTER TWENTY-SIX

HANSON HEARD NOVARRO mutter something. He couldn't make out the exact words, but from the tone it was a curse. He turned in his seat, keeping an easy hand on the wheel. Then he saw Novarro patting his pockets, like a man in need of tobacco.

"Cigar?" he asked.

Novarro forced a smile. "Please."

Hanson fished out his cigar case and laid it open. Novarro glanced, nodded absent thanks and took one. Hanson offered his knife, but Novarro waved it away. To Hanson's disgust, he bit off the end.

This pissed Hanson off. Fucking barbarian, he thought.

But as he did so, Novarro looked back—long and hard—at the receding boathouse. He spat the cigar nubbin over the side.

It was still twilight, which at that time of year would hang on for a while longer, but lights were necessary on the lake because of all the snags and sandbars—mudbars, really—quite capable of putting an unwary boater permanently out of action. A seven-year drought had dropped the lake's level to alarming lows in some places, leaving deep holes dug out by gators with shallow water all around—like island chains in reverse. Stumps and fallen trees poked up here and there, making things even more perilous.

Off to the left, Hanson saw an old abandoned houseboat, leaning crazily on its side half in and half out of the muck

The bodyguards' boat sped away from the dock, heading straight for Novarro's craft, big spotlight spearing across the water, picking out the bad parts and maneuvering around them. Hanson nodded-that's what Jose and Geraldo were supposed to do. Close with them then drop back and play rear guard while the little flotilla crossed the lake. Then they'd head into the long channel that led into the bay, where they'd all rendezvous with Captain Mirasol and his deep-water hovercraft.

Novarro stared intently at the approaching speedboat. Hanson could almost see the wheels turning behind his eyes. For some reason the boat was pissing him off.

Calm down, Novarro, he thought. We've got a lot of shit still to come. He felt better when Novarro lit the cigar and drew on it. That should do the job. Good Cuban smoke to lighten the soul.

Then Novarro's eyes narrowed and he exhaled a thick cloud.

The asshole didn't even take the time to taste the smoke, Hanson thought. Hundred-dollar fucking cigar, for crying out loud.

Novarro turned to him, eyes burning.

"God damn," he said. He threw the cigar over the side.

Hanson's muscles did an involuntary jump—he almost leaped after the little beauty. Then he looked up at Novarro, bewildered, and irritated to all hell at the waste.

"What the fuck's wrong?" he demanded.

"A bad feeling."

The answer was far from satisfactory- he was starting to think Novarro was letting mission nerves get the better of him. Moving with great deliberation, Hanson settled back in his seat, taking note of Novarro's reactions. He did a slow ten...nine...eight count so he could be certain his own nerves were under control.

Hanson could practically see Novarro run his suspicions through a hard mill of bad experiences. Then Novarro blinked—making his decision. He reached for the mike and punched the private frequency tabs. Hanson didn't have to thing hard to understand that Novarro was cutting out the guard boat and speaking to the other members of his water-borne security team.

Before he keyed the mike, he said, "As you gringos say: better safe than sorry." Then he depressed the long, fat side

Allan Cole

button. "We may have trouble, gentleman. I want three gunboats back with me."

When three of the main security boats broke from the pack and headed back Hanson started to worry. What the hell was wrong with Novarro? If they missed the rendezvous with Mirasol's ship they were fucked big time. They'd be sitting in the middle of the ocean with fifty half-drugged kids just coming out of it and whining and crying their hearts out. The goddamned Coast Guard would have them for breakfast, lunch, dinner and all the snacks in between.

He shaded his eyes and looked back to observe the approach of the worrisome boat. At this angle, the slowly setting tropical sun cast golden shadows across the water, making everything seem surreal, not to be trusted. But even through the glare he could see the suspicious boat closing on them.

Suspicious to Novarro, that is.

"Let's check them out," Novarro ordered, pointing at the approaching craft.

Hanson turned the wheel in a long lazy arc and at the same time he gave the engines a bit more good gas to drink, and the speedboat surged around and roared back the way they'd come.

*   *   *

Mac saw the maneuver and wondered what to do. For a time he kept the half-sunken houseboat between Novarro and himself, but that bit of shelter didn't last long.

He wracked his brains for inspiration. His Great-uncle Addison Mizner would have pulled some sort of a con, but he was moving too fast to salt a goldmine or stack a deck. His Great-uncle Ferris, sheriff of old Miami, would've stolen the ballots and headed for Tallahassee to elect a new brand of thieves to head Navarro off at the pass. If Mac's great-great-grandfather had still been the governor of Florida, he might have been able to pull it off. Assuming Mac had a time machine and cell phones could be made to work in the 19th Century.

He could call out the army. He was related to Andrew Jackson via a romantic liaison with a mulatto beauty during

Jackson's raids into Spanish Florida. One of his descendants was now a member of the Joint Chiefs Of Staff.

Shit, that's it, Mac thought. He just had to call Andy, and the whole damned 101st Airborne would show up. It would take some explaining, sure. But when he said it was kids, Andy would come through. He knew that about his cousin- with kids he'd say send the Army first, worry about apologizing later.

Mac put a palm across the useless cell phone in his pocket—Aw shit, no good. Fingered the radio unit next to the wheel. Could he get through?

He started to pick up the mike, but Novarro's voice cut in. Speaking in Spanish. Telling him to close up with the flotilla. He could see Novarro's craft dropping back to meet him, so there was nothing he could say or do, nor were then any tricks he pull out of his sleeve. Even if he could talk to the Joint Chiefs of Staff directly, it'd be all over before someone transcribed the conversation.

Just in case, he picked up the mike and keyed the radio, hoping against hope. Horrible squealing pierced his ears. He cut the unit. Novarro was jamming everything in the lake.

So much for the Big Red One.

There was only one other thing to do-fuck with their heads. Don't let them know until the very last instant that he was an army of one.

He ducked his head, took a good grip on the throttle and surged ahead to meet Novarro. His free hand crept out to find his gun-with a little luck he could get in a fortuitous shot, blow Novarro away and end it before things got out of control.

And he'd always been lucky, hadn't he?

*   *   *

Hanson was careful as he guided the craft toward the approaching vessel. On the one hand, he thought Novarro was being a suspicious shit. On the other, there was always that "better safe than sorry" line.

He glanced at the seat next to him to see if his weapon was in easy reach… It was.

130

Allan Cole

CHAPTER TWENTY-SEVEN

AS THEY CLOSED on the boat, Novarro leaned out, trying to see who was at the wheel. Hanson snorted. He thought the whole exercise was nonsense.

"We can't keep screwing around like this, Mr. Novarro," he said. "If we get caught out here with all those kids…Well, Jesus. Even the Company won't be able to cover our asses."

Novarro didn't seem to hear him. He said, low, almost to himself, "It's MacGregor…I'm sure of it."

Hanson couldn't stand it any longer. It was time to shit or get off the pot. He grabbed his Uzi and turned toward Mac's boat.

"If he shoots back, it's MacGregor," he said. "If he doesn't, he's ours."

And with that he opened fire, deliberately spraying just over the head of the shadowy figure at the wheel.

He waited.

Not more than two seconds.

Then he saw the shadowy figure jerk upward, and he and Novarro were diving for cover as Mac fired back.

"Shit, you're right… It's fucking MacGregor."

Novarro grabbed Hanson's weapon.

"Get back on the wheel," he snarled, and stood up in full sight and pressed the trigger.

*　　*　　*

Bullets shattered the windshield and slammed into the deck and sides. Mac kept his cool-he didn't duck or try to weave but concentrated on controlling the vessel. He pulled hard on the wheel, and the boat heeled over on its side, roaring away with a swarm of bullets following it like flies chasing a dying Key deer across a swamp.

He had no intention of becoming fly fodder. He cranked up the power and slammed ahead of his pursuers. Except, instead of running to hide in the reeds, he swept around in a tight arc and went after the main convoy that carried the children. The maneuver caught the others by surprise. For a few minutes—to his great satisfaction—his pursuers were all over the place, nearly colliding in their haste to get at him.

But the chaos was short-lived. Novarro was an able manager of death, and in a manner of minutes he had four gunboats on his tail, with Novarro in the lead.

*   *   *

Lupe heard the gunfire and turned to see what was going on, but the engine spray and violent motion made it impossible to make out what was happening. She was jammed in the stern, Leslie in her arms, surrounded by frightened and crying children. Not far away, Tampa hunched over the wheel, while Bonita rode shotgun in a seat to his left. Her eyes were continuously roving, her weapon following her eyes.

Lupe did her best to calm the kids, shushing them and singing little songs. The kids were mostly of Spanish origin, so she sang things like the Spanish Lullaby:

"...You're my beautiful melody
No querido estas sentir
Quien es mi amor
I can feel your love calling for me
De amor, de quiero
You're my Spanish lullaby..."

She didn't know if it helped- they were all woozy from the narcotics in their systems and a few had gotten sick.

The situation was threatening to overwhelm her. She felt pretty rocky herself from the combination of downers and uppers percolating in her system. But after years of pulling double shifts in her parking business, swigging high-octane Starbucks products, she had a tried-and-true trick to chase tiredness and even severe hangover from her body.

She simply refused to admit they existed.

This was what she did now—drawing in the fresh air blasting into her face to help give her willpower a boost. Dipping up lake water to douse her face, wetting a hanky to wash Leslie's—cleaning her up, making her new again to the best of her ability. Whispering words of encouragement to the little girl. Not knowing if she was getting through but trying just the same.

Like she had done all her life.

When things were bleak, the family down and failing, Lupe had always come through. Got the education to improve on the economic shield her father had built. Took over the business and really made something out of it. Financed her brothers and sisters and cousins in other small businesses. After floating on a tire inside her mother's tummy, Lupe was determined her whole family was going to make it come hell or high water.

And right now, her family consisted of Leslie and any other kid she could get free.

Then she heard gunfire and turned in time to see Bonita's head jerk up, shotgun rising with the motion. Once again, Lupe looked back to see what was what.

Tampa maneuvered to stay with the rest of the convoy, and his long curve shifted the curtain of spray to one side. Suddenly Lupe could make out the action behind them. A speedboat rushed down on the convoy, followed by four other gunboats which poured a steady stream of gunfire.

The figure at the wheel of the boat closing in on them wasn't trying to fire back or defend himself-he just poured on the power, trying to catch up. Leslie must have been watching as well, because she said, "What is it, Lupe?" Her little voice was very excited.

Lupe knew the answer.

"It's Mac," she said, hugging her close.

"I knew it," Leslie chortled. "I knew it. I knew it."

Then Mac's boat put on even more speed and surged up alongside theirs. Lupe could see him clearly now.

She waved.

"Here, Mac," she shouted. "Over here."

He saw her, waved back then edged his boat closer until they were rail to rail. Steadying the wheel with one hand, he gingerly got one foot up on the rail.

Lupe held her breath. He was going to jump. He balanced, getting ready to leap.

Just then Bonita spotted him.

"Christ, it's the asshole," she shouted.

Tampa saw him and whipped the wheel over so the nose rammed Mac's boat. At the same time, Bonita let loose with her shotgun.

*   *   *

Mac dropped back on the deck, a huge hole torn through the rail where he had been balanced a moment before. Then another shotgun blast ripped up the deck next to him.

With no one at the wheel of Mac's craft, and Tampa slamming into it, the boat skidded out of control. Any second and it would flip end over end.

Mac fought to his knees and grappled with the wheel. He managed to get the boat steady, but by then he had dropped far behind Lupe and Leslie.

There came the stutter of machinegun fire, and holes were stitched across the side. He bulled onward, craning his head around to see Novarro and the others charging down on him.

He veered to the side, drawing them away from the convoy. Then he suddenly swept back, trying for Lupe and Leslie once again.

Except he hadn't counted on the guard boats still traveling with the convoy.

One of them—acting on Novarro's radioed orders— suddenly turned and burst out of the pack, leaping over the churned-up surface. Behind him, Novarro and the others moved to close the jaws of the trap.

Then Mac saw a ski jump ahead. He whipped the wheel over, gave it all the throttle he had and shot up the ramp. He went up, up, hurtling off the ramp and over the lake. His outboard engine barely cleared the other boat; then he hit the water and charged onward.

Mac's pursuer nearly rammed into Novarro's boat, but Hanson got out of the way just in time. Even so, Mac had

Allan Cole

created a momentary tangle among his enemies, and once again he was in the clear and heading for the convoy.

Unfortunately, Novarro and the others had his range now. Soon as they were clear, Novarro quickly got them into formation, and as the chase continued, they opened fire.

Bullets crashed all around Mac, slowly ripping his boat to pieces. Then, up ahead he spotted a finger of land—a narrow peninsula—sticking into the lake. A huge banyan tree hung out over the water. He steered for it, slowing down, drawing Novarro and the others with him.

Mac wasn't quite sure how he was going to work this, but then he saw something moving deep in the shadows of the tree. He was in luck. He slowed more and soon he was ducking down as bullets poured in from the nearest speedboats.

Just as the first branches closed over him, he goosed the throttle, charging forward until he saw the source of the movement. It was a mud wallow deep in the tangle of the banyan's roots and half a dozen wild pigs squealed in anger and alarm as he came at them. Some fled. The big boars stood their ground, wheeling around to face him, their heavy tusks winking in the dim light.

At the last minute, Mac turned the wheel as sharply as he could. His boat skimmed past the wallow, close enough so that one of the pigs charged him and he felt the boat shudder under the impact. Then he was free, slashing through the branches and back out into the lake.

Behind him, some of Novarro's men weren't so lucky. Shouting with glee when they thought they had Mac cornered, they didn't hear the pigs over the big engines.

Mac veered away and they were suddenly confronted by the boars. Their boat slammed into the wallow, burying its nose in the mud. The pigs charged aboard, ripping and tearing at the crew.

Out in the lake Mac winced when he heard their screams. Then he gave his boat more gas and sped after the convoy.

CHAPTER TWENTY-EIGHT

THE SUN WAS making a slow dip over the mainland when the children's convoy entered the channel that led from the lake out into the open sea. Microphone in hand, Novarro kept an eye on Mac's boat—which was far behind the convoy now—while barking orders to his men.

"Cut him off," he shouted, waving them forward. "Cut him off."

Two of his boats closed on Mac from either side. Gunmen rose to catch Mac in a deadly crossfire.

* * *

Mac couldn't hear a damn thing over the roar of his own engine, but he sensed his peril. Just as Novarro's men opened up, he suddenly chopped the power. The other boats blasted ahead, and there were shouts of alarm and screams of pain as the men became the victims of their own trap. One of the boats lost it, flipping on its side, shattering and—sending pieces of Fiberglass skipping across the lake's surface like pebbles thrown by boys.

Mac slammed on the gas and was off again. The two remaining boats—Novarro's in the lead—stayed hot on his tail.

Far ahead, the convoy was breaking out of the channel and heading into the open sea. More lights came on as night drew nearer. Mac gripped the wheel, leaning forward, whispering: "Come on, come on, come on."

Waves rolled in from the Atlantic, and the boat was pounded from bow to stern. Mac used all his hard-won knowledge of the sea to win a slight edge over the others, hitting waves just so, turning his craft in subtle ways that helped the big engines deal with the rolling seas. For a while it worked, and he slowly pulled ahead of his enemies for no other reason than his passage was smoother.

Then he grabbed a look and saw that his pursuers had finally caught on and were quickly closing the gap again.

* * *

Captain Mirasol watched the convoy coming toward him through a pair of binoculars. He lowered them and turned to Lt. Aru, who was at the wheel.

"Our clients approach."

Lt. Aru shook his head. "I am not...comfortable with this, Captain," he said. "After all...we're talking about...children...innocent children."

Captain Mirasol tried to look cheerful. "I'm told that most of them come from terrible homes... Perhaps our patrons are offering them a better life."

"Somehow, I don't think so," Aru said.

"Oh, you don't know what a bad life for a child is," Mirasol replied. "Your mother spoiled you. Trust me. They'll be better off. And as for the end result—from long experience I can promise you'll feel much happier when you deposit the bonus our employers have pledged."

The young lieutenant tried to look agreeable. Mirasol, after all, was not only his captain but first cousin to his mother. Aru's family was deep in debt because of certain thieves who had descended on them after his father died, and Captain Mirasol had given him a chance to earn their way out from under.

He nodded and returned to his work. But try as he could, he didn't feel, much less look, reassured.

Mirasol caught his mood and frowned.

* * *

As they approached the hovercraft, Lupe clutched Leslie close. The strange-looking ship, which sat very long and very low in the water like some kind of stealth craft from the Persian Gulf Wars, was menacing in the extreme.

The water became choppier when they left the lake and pushed into the ocean. Now nearly all of the children were sick. Trying to tend to them was so overwhelming she finally just had to give up. She held Leslie, and they whispered cheery things to each other, pretending to be Brownies on a weekend outing.

Lupe couldn't believe how together Leslie was. How steady her nerves were. She'd apparently suffered some sort of a bad reaction the first time Mrs. Cortez had sedated her, but it didn't seem to have done any permanent harm. She was tired, of course. And frightened. Hell, Lupe was scared to death. Who wouldn't be?

Still, she was fairly confident the child wouldn't spoil things if there was the slightest chance of escape.

She kept looking back, hoping to see Mac again, but she couldn't make out which of the small dots was his boat and which were the pursuers.

As if reading her mind, Leslie said, "Where's Uncle Mac? Can you see him?"

"No, I can't, honey."

Leslie patted her. "Don't worry," she soothed. "He'll come. I know he will."

"Sure, honey, sure," Lupe agreed,—trying very hard to believe.

*   *   *

Things weren't going so well for Mac. His boat had been shot to pieces and smoke was pouring out of the engine compartment. To make matters worse, Novarro's craft was streaking toward him from the left, and the other gunboat was coming at him from the right.

When his enemies were in position, they opened up, and this time there was no escaping the deadly crossfire. Mac hunched down, a hail of bullets chewing up what was left of his boat. It seemed to him there were so many holes in it that only pure speed was keeping it from sinking.

He had a mad thought. What if he suddenly cut the engine? Would he crash dive to the bottom like a submarine? He laughed. What a joke on Novarro that would be. The only drowning fly in the swimming pool was that, to accomplish the joke, he would have to die.

One of those vague notions came to him that occur to people suddenly faced with their possible demise. When everything goes to shit, dive as deep as you can.

He held on to that notion like it was pure gold.

138

Allan Cole

* * *

Novarro was starting to feel good about the day for the first time. He was a good marksman-almost a great marksman—and had been an alternate on the Olympic shooting team when he was a foreign exchange cadet at VMI.

Novarro had by now calmed enough to really study how MacGregor handled his boat. Once they'd entered the open sea, Mac had been forced to be very deliberate about his movements - not only to stay ahead but to weather the heavy waves. Before this moment, Novarro had tried to kill MacGregor, not his boat. Now he realized his error. Focusing on a larger target—especially a moving one—made more sense.

He took slow, determined aim. His sights found the place where he knew the gas tank would be. A wave ran under his boat, and the nose bumped up, throwing off his aim.

"Steady," he hissed at Hanson.

Hanson held it steady.

He found the gas tank again and, without hesitating, trusted his instinct and fired.

Mac's boat became a ghastly ball of flame and black smoke. Novarro gloated at the fiery rain—the fallout from Mac's destroyed boat that drifted down, hissing, into the sea.

"May you burn in Hell, MacGregor," he said.

"Amen to that, brother," Hanson agreed.

* * *

Lupe bit back a moan of despair. She clutched Leslie and turned away so the child would be spared the sight.

* * *

Hanson circled the blazing pool of gas, oil and burning debris. Novarro looked over the side, making sure his nemesis was dead. He examined every board, every clump of open space between the burning pools of oil.

A feeling of great accomplishment stole over him.

"Fuck you, MacGregor," he said.

Then he signaled Hanson and they roared off toward the hovercraft.

* * *

After many long seconds Mac's head emerged through the space between two burning seat cushions. The smell and the smoke were terrible, and he pushed the cushions away, coughing. He wondered if he had any lining left in his lungs.

He tried some deep breathing exercises, coughing at first, then gradually drawing in the air more easily. Good thing I quit smoking, he thought. Then he considered the task before him and wished to hell he had a cigarette.

Treading water, he paddled around, getting oriented. Off in the distance he saw Novarro's boat. It was approaching something he had never seen before except in magazines—a big damned ocean-going hovercraft.

He started swimming for it with long, slow, powerful strokes.

Allan Cole

CHAPTER TWENTY-NINE

TAMPA AND BONITA boosted the Latina chick and the kid she was hanging on to up the ladder. He felt surly and out of sorts.

"That's the last of 'em," he said.

Bonita caught his mood. "What's the matter, sweetie-pie?"

He hesitated then took the plunge.

"Well, we never talked about it, you know?"

Bonita looked at him. "Talked about what, hon?"

"Kids," Tampa said. "You never said if you wanted any."

She burst into laughter. "Is that what was worrying you?... Don't be ridiculous. Remember—we've got a strict no-kid's rule at the RV park. And I not only intend to keep it that way, I intend to set a good example to our tenants."

Tampa grinned hugely. "God, I love ya', baby," he said.

* * *

Novarro's boat slid up to the hovercraft. He and Hanson scrambled up the side while crewmen from the hovercraft secured it. On the bridge, he found Mirasol and Aru waiting.

"I want to get underway immediately," he ordered.

Mirasol nodded and turned to Aru.

"You know what to do, lieutenant."

Aru gave him a smart salute then exited the bridge to do his captain's bidding, but his manner was that of an unhappy man.

Novarro and Hanson looked after him.

"Your first officer seems troubled, Captain," Novarro said.

"He's young, that's all... He only wants a little seasoning."

Hanson laughed. "He'll get all the seasoning he needs this trip," he said. "It's not often you smuggle people out of the good old US of A."

Mirasol smiled. "That is a most excellent observation."

*   *   *

Night had fallen, but a bright moon illuminated gentle seas. The hovercraft's big engines were idling—a comforting sound to those who wanted to leave, a frightening drum roll for the victims. Adding to that, whether comforting or ominous, was the bustle of the crew as they hauled in the ladders and slammed and secured the hull doors.

The hovercraft stirred, water boiling up from its props, a loose line that had been somehow forgotten borne up by the troubled waters to trail lazily behind the ship.

The hovercraft moved slowly forward, but before orders were given to pick up speed there was a sudden flash of white water at its stern. Then another.

Mac emerged.

He spotted the line and put on a burst of muscle power, grabbing the rope and hauling himself in. The hovercraft started to go faster, rising higher. He got a tighter grip on the line and heaved out of the water. He started climbing hand-over-hand up the sides.

Then the ship throttled full forward and came all the way out of the water on its rails at top speed. He was slammed back and forth, and it was all he could do to not be shaken off into the roiling seas below.

Finally, the hovercraft's speed smoothed out and he stopped swinging. He paused a moment, catching his breath, then planted his feet, shifted his grip and walked up the sides.

On the main deck two of Novarro's men were lugging a wooden box. Red paint warned of its contents: DANGER: EXPLOSIVES. They carried the box into the bridge area. When they were gone, Mac popped up over the rail. He looked about, saw no one and slipped over onto the deck.

Footsteps approached, and he ducked out of sight just as two more explosives-carrying crewmen came on deck.

*   *   *

142

Allan Cole

Down in the main cargo hold, where Lupe and Leslie and the children had been locked away, Mrs. Cortez sat at a makeshift desk, going over her dosage charts. The hovercraft hit a rough patch and some of the children whimpered.

Mrs. Cortez turned her steely gaze toward the sound, eyes sweeping the forms huddled on sleeping bags spread out in even rows across the deck. When they realized she was watching them, the children stopped their whimpering and Mrs. Cortez turned back to her notes. When they reached their destination she would need these detailed records to get them ready. Like cleaning out freshly gathered mussels - feed them a lot of oatmeal for a few days and their organs would be purged clean and glistening.

Bonita and Tampa guarded the entrance to the hold. It was boring duty, and they amused themselves poring over RV brochures.

*   *   *

Lupe carefully observed the trio. By now she knew who everyone was, including the cracker, Tampa, and his Latina girlfriend, Bonita. When she was sure their attention was elsewhere, she leaned down to whisper to Leslie.

"We'll have to get out of here on our own, Leslie... But it's probably going to be scary, okay?"

Leslie's answer was firm: "Scary is waiting for more bad things to happen. I don't want to do that anymore."

Lupe hugged her. "Then we won't."

Again, she glanced to see that Mrs. Cortez and Tampa and Bonita were occupied. Then she nodded to Leslie, and the two started to slide inch by inch along the wall toward a side exit. As if sensing motion, Mrs. Cortez suddenly turned in their direction. Her steel-framed glasses glinted in the overhead light.

They froze.

Finally, she went back to her work, and they started moving again.

When they reached the door, Lupe hesitated, checking to see if everything was safe. She eased her hand up to the latch. Leslie watched, wide-eyed.

A loudspeaker crackled into life.

"Cargo hold," boomed Novarro's voice. "Report."

Mrs. Cortez lifted her head and answered, "The children have all had their tranquilizers and seasickness medicine, Señor Novarro. They're all very quiet now."

"I don't want to take any chances with them, Mrs. Cortez," he said. "Please do what is necessary."

"Yes, Señor Novarro… I have the injections prepared. Now that they are tranquil, it will be easy to administer the sleeping medicine."

"Very good, Mrs. Cortez." Novarro clicked off.

Mrs. Cortez opened a box filled with syringes and started setting up a tray. Bonita and Tampa went back to RV shopping.

Lupe kept a protective arm around Leslie, and waited as Mrs. Cortez finished loading the tray then rose to administer injections. This was getting complicated. They couldn't leave, but if they waited too long they'd be rendered incapable of escape.

She felt Leslie quiver. The same thoughts were probably running through the child's mind. The little girl was sure a trooper – especially for a ten-year-old. Her grandmother, Stormy, might have a lurid past, but she certainly had done well by Leslie.

"Just a little longer," she whispered.

The girl nodded and cuddled closer.

Allan Cole

CHAPTER THIRTY

COURSE SET FOR Honduras, the hovercraft moved through the night at an amazing rate of speed. Perched on its wide rails, it flew like a swift shadow under the bright moon. Several crewmen moved about the deck then, one-by-one, disappeared inside. When they were gone, Mac slipped out of hiding and crept toward the bridge.

He'd taken no more than a few steps when one of Navarro's gunmen came around the corner and headed in his direction. He hid behind a tied-down Zodiac and waited for him to pass. The moment he did, Mac came up, grabbing his hair with one hand and ramming his knuckles into the man's kidneys, silencing him before he could even squeak. He pinched the carotid artery, shutting off the blood flow, until the gunman was unconscious then lowered him quietly to the deck.

Mac quickly stripped the man of his weapons and ammo and dragged him behind one of the Zodiacs. He bound and gagged the guy, rolling him under one of the rubber-sided boats. When he was done, he checked once again to see if anyone was about then crept toward the bridge, weapon at the ready.

*   *   *

Lupe and Leslie lay curled up by the door, pretending to sleep as Mrs. Cortez injected the children with sleeping potion. A few of them cried when she pricked their arms, but she told them to shush and they quickly fell asleep.

She worked her way down the row until she finally came to a child sprawled next to Lupe. She set the tray of hypodermics down on the floor.

As she swabbed the little boy's arm with alcohol, Lupe shot out her hand and snatched a hypo from the tray. Then she closed her eyes and pretended to be asleep. Mrs. Cortez moved over to her, a new hypo ready, but instead of injecting Lupe she moved past her to inject Leslie first. The child trembled, and Lupe was afraid she was going to cry out, but she kept her eyes firmly shut.

When Mrs. Cortez leaned down to administer the dose, Lupe popped up behind her, put a strong hand across her mouth and jabbed her in the throat with the needle. The woman struggled fiercely, but Lupe held on until she became groggy and weak. Then she kept the woman's mouth and nose covered until she passed out.

Finally, she lowered Mrs. Cortez to the deck. She looked over at Tampa and Bonita, but the engine noises had drowned out the struggle and besides they were too busy with their magazine to notice anything thing.

Smiling, she gave Leslie a hug. "That was great, honey. What an actress you're going to make."

Leslie giggled

Then Lupe said, "We're going to try it now, okay?"

The girl nodded, and Lupe reached up very slowly to lift the bar lever on the door. At the same time, she leaned her weight against it.

To her horror, the moment the door came open an alarm blared into life. The sound was deafening as horns hooted all over the ship.

"Never mind that," she yelled and pulled Leslie through the opening.

*   *   *

Tampa and Bonita looked up in time to see the woman and child bolt through the door and slam it behind them. Bonita started after them, but Tampa lagged back.

"Come on, hon," she shouted. "Let's go."

He glowered.

"Nobody better bite me this time," he said.

"If they do," Bonita said, "shoot their asses!"

Tampa grinned-that made him feel better. They raced after the fugitives.

*   *   *

Allan Cole

On the bridge, Novarro and the others were jolted by the sound of the alarm. No one had to ask what it meant.

"I want every man on this," Novarro said to Mirasol. "Lock this ship up so tight a roach couldn't escape."

"Not to worry, Señor," Mirasol assured him. "There's nowhere to run—unless they want to take their chances with the sharks."

Hanson spotted something outside and pointed.

"Shit," he said. "What the hell's that?"

Everyone looked. Through the bridge's window they could see a helicopter searchlight sweeping across the water.

Captain Mirasol wasn't bothered. He shrugged.

"Only the Coast Guard," he said. "Probably on a routine patrol. Nothing to do with us, I'm sure. After all, no one knows there's anything to look for on my ship. And even if they did—there's too much traffic out there to find us."

Hanson got it. He chuckled.

"Friggin' Coast Guard," he said. "Everybody at the Agency knows that the Coast Guard has its nose permanently up its behind."

"Even so," Novarro said, "I'm glad I thought to take out a little insurance."

He moved to a tarp-covered gurney in the corner and threw the tarp aside, revealing the boxes of explosives the men had lugged aboard. A small black detonation device sat next to them. He lifted it up, indicating the toggle switch.

"If they try to interfere with us," he said, "we'll have fifty young hostages to keep them at bay. And if they play me false, I will not hesitate to throw the switch."

Aru stared at the box. He licked dry lips.

"But won't you kill us all as well?" he said.

Novarro snorted. "What do you take me for? This is a remote. We'll stand off a nice safe distance when we do the job. Assuming it's even necessary, of course. However, I'm with Captain Mirasol. I don't think there's much likelihood we'll be interfered with."

"Hell, no," Hanson agreed. "Nobody even knows we're out here."

*   *   *

Aboard the helicopter, Lt. Snow and Albert peered into the night, following the track of the big searchlight. They saw nothing but empty seas broken only by the occasional fishing craft or party boat.

"They could be anywhere, Albert," she said.

"But—fifty kids," he protested. "That's a lot to hide. They'd have something pretty big."

The Coast Guard pilot – Lt. Sean Moon - made a noise of derision.

"Fifty is nothing, sir," he said. I've seen twice that number of refugees crammed into little more than a skiff. When it comes to people-smuggling, the bastards can get real creative." Moon shuddered at some memory. "Real creative," he repeated.

"I just hope to hell Mac's out there," Lt. Snow said. "We need somebody to start whittling down the odds for us."

Mad Albert nodded. "Mac's good at that."

*   *   *

Mac rose up from hiding behind the superstructure of the hovercraft's bridge and saw the helicopter spotlight sweeping over the water. He grinned in relief-Albert must've made it after all.

The grin vanished when he saw the chopper start moving away in another direction.

He looked frantically around, then spotted a red emergency box bolted to the wall of the bridge. He rushed to it, clawed it open and got out the flare gun. He pointed it over his head and fired into the night sky.

*   *   *

Novarro jumped like he'd been stabbed when he saw a red flare explode high over the bow.

"MacGregor," he snarled.

"That's crazy," Hanson said. "He's dead. I saw him burn the hell up."

Novarro pulled a machine pistol from under his jacket and ratcheted in a round.

"Make no mistake," he insisted. "It's MacGregor."

He raced out the door.

148

Allan Cole

Hanson shook his head, but even so, he drew his own gun and followed, muttering, "That son of a bitch has more lives than friggin' Fidel Castro.

CHAPTER THIRTY-ONE

LUPE AND LESLIE raced along a dim passageway, trying one door after another, looking for a place to hide. All the doors were locked.

Behind them, they heard Bonita shout, "There they are."

Someone opened fire and Leslie shrieked as a bullet slammed into the metal wall next to them but Lupe kept going, pulling the little girl after her. More bullets followed, but she ducked around corner and for a moment they were out of the line of fire. To her dismay, the way was blocked by heavy steel doors.

She clawed at the lever, and to her vast relief it turned and the door swung open. They dashed through and pushed it shut just as another bullet slammed into it.

*   *   *

Tampa yanked at the handle, but as he did, he heard a "click" as their quarry locked the door.

"God damn it all to hell."

He aimed his pistol at the lock and fired—Boom! Boom! Boom! but the bullets only ricocheted off the metal and zinged all around, bouncing off the walls and buzzing by them like murderous wasps. He and Bonita instinctively covered their heads until the ricocheting stopped. Miraculously, they were unscathed.

"Sorry, hon," he said weakly.

Bonita only shook her head. She went to a fire cabinet, opened the door and pulled out a fire extinguisher. She examined the label, nodded, and lugged it back to the door.

"Watch it, hon," she warned. "This is liquid nitrogen. It'll burn the be-Jesus out of you."

Tampa stepped back and she let loose a frigid blast at the lock. When the steel had turned nearly blue with cold she nodded at him.

"Hit it with something," she said. "And I don't mean a bullet."

Tampa reversed his gun and smacked the lock. It shattered like glass. He beamed at her.

"Baby, you're the greatest," he said.

Bonita shrugged. "My mother was in the Merchant Marines," she said.

*　　*　　*

Lupe and Leslie crept through a hold packed with freight of all kinds—from machine parts to farm equipment. The equipment sat in disordered rows eight to ten feet high with narrow aisles separating them.

Leslie wrinkled her nose at the sour smell of the creosote used to protect the freight from salt spray. Then she gave a little shriek as somewhere behind them a door was flung open and light burst in.

Lupe dragged her behind cover just in time as someone opened fire, bullets slamming against the metal deck and ricocheting off the machinery.

They scrambled along a narrow on their hands and knees. Heavy machines loomed over them. As they burrowed into their hiding place they heard their pursuers race toward them.

Lupe pulled the girl down as flashlight beams scooted past their bolt hole. Then Lupe's heart jumped as the light returned, spearing down the narrow aisle. There," she heard Bonita shout.

Lupe leaped to her feet and pulled Leslie with her as a flashlight beam speared them.

She had time to see Tampa raise his weapon, then ducked behind a tractor as he opened up- full auto, this time. Lupe and Leslie cowered behind the tractor as bullets crashed all around them.

The moment they stopped, she grabbed the girl and they crawled away into the darkness.

Footsteps approached. Then a flashlight beam speared down the aisle, but the fugitives got out of the way just in time.

"I think they went this way," they heard Tampa said.

Crouched under a skip-loader, they listened as the pair moved down the aisle. They saw legs start by then hesitate for a long, agonizing moment. Then they heard Bonita say, "Down there."

Footsteps headed away from them and they breathed sighs of relief.

After the hunters were gone, they scurried across the aisle to the other side.

* * *

Mac dropped behind a Zodiac as a fusillade of automatic weapons fire spattered all around him. The Zodiac's inflated rubber sides gave out a loud whoosh as the vessel collapsed-he had to practically dig his nose into the deck to avoid the steady stream of fire.

Then the remaining bulk of the Zodiac started taking the hits, and he thanked the gods of high-speed boats for coming up with such a remarkably sturdy craft.

* * *

Out on the main deck, Novarro and Hanson supervised the attack. Three gunman moved ahead of them as Novarro scoped the situation. He knew damned well that Mac was behind the ruined Zodiac, but what would he do next? He quickly gave the guessing game up and took the easier way out.

"Ten thousand dollars to the man who puts a bullet in that bastardo!"

The gunnies grinned. He'd gotten their attention, all right. Then they became very serious-checking their weapons, their supply of ammo. He was about to curse them to get a move on when they all ducked down low and started toward the Zodiac. They hadn't gone more than a few feet when Mac popped up, fired two rounds and dropped down again.

The men dove to the deck as if those two bullets had been a firestorm from a regiment. They tried a feeble rally, returning fire, rising up and making a ragged dash for the Zodiac. When there was no return fire Novarro knew Mac was gone.

152

Allan Cole

It took the gunnies a few minutes to realize that, however. They edged around the Zodiac, weapons and nerves on hair trigger. Then their self-appointed leader rose up and turned to Novarro. He didn't say anything—just gave an embarrassed shrug.

"Get after him," Novarro shouted. "And the price is now twenty thousand."

The gunnies took heart at this news and leaped to do his bidding. They disappeared into the hold after Mac.

Novarro and Hanson started after them, but suddenly they heard the roar of an approaching helicopter. A few seconds later a searchlight beam swept across the deck then froze on the superstructure of the bridge. Even though it wasn't focused on them, the light was so intense they had to shield their eyes with their hands.

A loudspeaker crackled into life, and a voice boomed out, "This is the U.S. Coast Guard. Prepare to be boarded!"

CHAPTER THIRTY-TWO

AS THE COAST GUARD chopper's searchlight swept the deck, Novarro and Hanson ducked behind the Zodiac Mac had just abandoned.

"Take care of MacGregor," Novarro said. "I'll deal with the Coast Guard."

Hanson nodded and hurried off. Novarro rushed to the railing and braced himself. Then he raised his machine pistol and fired a long stream of bullets at the helicopter.

*   *   *

Lt. Aru and Captain Mirasol shielded their eyes against the spotlight's glare. They heard the chatter of Novarro's gunfire and saw the chopper veer away.

Shaken, Aru turned back to the wheel. "Now we shall pay for what we are doing to those children."

Mirasol didn't reply. His face became quite pale and his sad eyes even sadder. He went to a drawer, slid it open and took out a gun.

Lt. Aru saw the gun and frowned. "What are you doing with that, Captain?" he demanded. "When the Coast Guard boards the last thing we should do is offer resistance."

Mirasol sighed. "I just can't take the chance, Lieutenant," he said. "I'm so sorry."

He shot Aru, and the young lieutenant slumped over the wheel. Mirasol sighed again, pocketed the pistol then hoisted Aru's body and dragged him toward the door.

Novarro opened the door and saw what was going on. "I see your young lieutenant didn't work out as well as you had hoped," he said.

"I'm afraid not," Mirasol replied. Then, very politely: "Will you hold the door, please?"

Novarro nodded and propped the door open while Mirasol muscled Aru out to the rail's edge. Then he heaved, dumping Aru onto the deck below. He shook his head then returned inside to the take charge of the wheel.

"It was my fault," he said, "He was too good. His mother wanted him to be a priest, but he liked the girls too much, you know?"

Novarro nodded—he knew.

"Don't blame yourself," he advised. "It was his youth that killed him."

Mirasol smiled a sad smile of agreement. Novarro went to the explosives and threw the tarp back.

"The real tragedy has yet to occur, my friend," he said. "I'm afraid I'm going to have to cut my losses and run."

Mirasol glanced at the explosives. His brows furrowed as he considered. Then he asked, "Do I have an invitation to run with you?"

"But of course, Captain," Novarro replied. "And I don't expect you to suffer for this setback financially, either. I need men of your talents to set up this operation again. It's too lucrative...too creative...to let fall by the wayside so easily."

Mirasol started feeling better, even philosophical. "Men will pay millions for the secret of youth."

"Actually, it isn't much of a secret anymore," Novarro said. "It can be had for the taking. You just have to have the nerve to cut it out of them."

Mirasol pointed out the window at the helicopter, whose lights were again moving toward the hovercraft.

"Our friends are returning, Senor. With reinforcements, no doubt."

Novarro looked, then busied himself with the explosives.

"I just have to put a few finishing touches to this," he said, "and I'll be ready."

*   *   *

Aru stirred. His eyes opened and he coughed; blood flecked his lips. He knew he was dying, but he forced himself to concentrate.

"I can't let them..." he whispered.

Going on sheer will power, he pushed himself to his knees. Aru saw the large yellow-striped tanks marked FUEL STORAGE.

He crawled toward the tanks.

*   *   *

Bonita caught the sound of running feet coming from a nearby hold. She signaled to Tampa and the two crept up to the dark doorway. In the distance she spotted a glowing red "Exit" sign. The light spilled eerily out across row upon row of steel racks. The smell of well-oiled metal emanated from the hold.

Then she saw two shadows moving swiftly along the center aisle – one small, one larger. It was the kid and the woman.

Bonita nodded at Tampa and they opened fire. Bullets crashed against the metal racks, drawing off long tongues of spark. There was a squeal from the little girl and Tampa cursed as their prey managed to duck behind one of the high metal racks.

"Never mind, sweetie," Bonita soothed. "We got them now."

They moved down the aisle, heading for the place where the pair had vanished. Scurrying footsteps alerted them to the fact that their prey was on the move, keeping the racks between them and the hunters.

Bonita wasn't bothered. She was certain they'd head for that "Exit" sign. What other chance did they have? Besides, there was nothing to fear from those two. They weren't even armed.

She noticed that the racks contained tools, mostly of the kind used by the crew to move the cargo around. They weren't locked down, like the racks in other areas, but loosely held by wide, gray elastic bands.

Bonita signaled to Tampa, who came closer. She pushed against one of the racks and rocked it from side to side. There was an involuntary gasp of terror from the other side and Tampa let go, spraying bullets through the open spaces.

Sensing that he'd missed, Bonita bent down and looked through one of the lower racks. She didn't see anything, but she thought she heard the faint patter of running feet. She fired, spraying bullets through the rack again. Then she

156

Allan Cole

stopped again to listen. She heard what she thought was a groan of pain.

Tampa beamed. "I think you got 'em, hon," he said.

Just as he spoke there was a long, loud ripping sound as ties gave away and then the rack started to tilt over. They tried to leap to the side, but the rack came crashing down, and they were buried by hundreds of tools.

Bonita managed to dodge most of tools and came up in time to see the two bolting for the exit again. Tampa shouted angrily and leaped to his feet, pushing tools aside. Before he let his temper get the better of him and rush off, Bonita grabbed him.

"The guns," she said, pointing at the debris.

Quickly, they found their weapons and took off after the pair. But before they got very far the woman paused long enough to heave over another tool rack and it crashed into their path.

"God damn," Tampa shouted, dodging as a large electric motor narrowly missed his head. Then a screwdriver fell point first and buried itself into the toe of his boot, missing his toes but standing straight up out of the leather.

Tampa marveled at it, then leaned down and plucked it out. He examined the screwdriver, then the hole in his boot top, considering…

* * *

Outside the cargo area Mac was moving along the passageway, when he heard a large crash. He stopped, then went to the corridor wall and pressed his ear against it.

He heard a man, with a Florida cracker accent say, "God damn, baby, will you look at this."

A woman replied, "Come on, sweetie! They're heading for the exit."

Mac looked up and saw a door far down the corridor. He hurried toward it.

CHAPTER THIRTY-THREE

LUPE AND LESLIE made it to the door. Lupe clawed at the handle, but just then their pursuers burst into view. They fired, and Leslie screamed as bullets chewed into the metal deck at her feet.

Suddenly, the door came open, and a hand shot out and dragged her through. Before Lupe could react the same hand returned and grabbed her by the waistband of her jeans and yanked her outside. The door slammed shut, a hail of gunfire slamming against the metal.

* * *

Tampa tried the door, but it was locked. He thought a minute then smiled.

"All's we need is another of them fire extinguishers, hon."

* * *

Lupe and Leslie embraced Mac.

"Oh, my God," Lupe cried. "You did come. You did come."

"I told you he would," Leslie said.

Mac heard something worrisome and untangled himself.

"This way," he said, leading them to a storage room. He opened the door and motioned them inside. "I'll be back for more kisses and hugs in a minute."

He shut the door and retraced his steps. He stopped at the cargo hold door, where he heard somebody pounding at the door lever, which Mac had locked. Whatever was being done to the lock didn't seem to be having much affect. Mac shrugged and moved along the corridor to the bend, where he again stopped to listen. He heard booted feet approaching. He raised his weapon and aimed at the wall—but at a sharp angle. Then he let loose.

Bullets struck the opposite wall and ricocheted around the bend.

* * *

Hanson and his gunnies hit the deck as a vertical rain of bullets crashed down the corridor. When the fusillade stopped, Hanson rolled to the side, came up on one knee and returned fire, stealing the trick and angling his weapon, going for the lucky ricochet kill. He stopped firing, listening for some response. Nothing. He dropped the clip, slammed in another and once again fired a withering burst. This time when he stopped to reload he heard the sound of footsteps running away.

He jumped to his feet, shouting, "We've got him on the run, boys!"

The gunnies leaped up, cursing and shouting defiantly. Hanson waved them on, and they raced around the corner, the CIA man right behind them. He came around the bend then skittered to a halt, surprised as all hell.

Standing about fifty feet away—bold as you please— was MacGregor.

He was positioned just on the other side of a closed door that led into the cargo hold, one hand on the lever that operated the door, the other holding a gun that was leveled at his pursuers. For some reason he wasn't firing.

Out of ammo, Hanson wondered?

His men were just as surprised, standing there not doing a thing except gape.

"Shoot, damn it! Shoot!" he thundered.

His men obeyed, coming out of that long frozen moment to let loose a hailstorm of lead. Mac suddenly jerked the cargo door open, jumping behind it to use as a shield.

* * *

Tampa and Bonita came tumbling out, guns blazing. But Tampa was hit by Hanson's crew and fell to the deck. Bonita dropped to her knees, crouching over him like a momma lion.

She turned burning eyes on Hanson and his men and screamed, "You killed Tampa, you sons of bitches!"

And she let loose with her gun. There was a blaze of back-and-forth fire. Bonita was so fierce that, although she was outnumbered, for a brief time she had the upper hand, mowing down gunnies like swamp weed. Even Hanson was hit, although not mortally

* * *

Hanson finally managed to get off a lucky shot. It ripped through Bonita's throat, killing her instantly. She fell across Tampa, her blood spreading on his chest.

Tampa's eyes opened. They widened when he saw Bonita's face inches from his own. He reached out a hand, touching her.

"Bonita, hon?" he cried, voice full of anguish. "Oh, God, hon. Don't be dead, baby. Don't be dead."

Then a shadow fell across him, and Tampa looked up. It was Hanson, weaving, dazed, looking down at what had happened.

"What the hell did you do that for?" Tampa shouted.

His gun came up and he fired point blank into Hanson's face. The CIA man was slammed back against the wall. And then he slumped to the floor, dead.

Tampa tried to kiss Bonita, but he was too weak to move his head.

"I got him baby," he blubbered. "I got him."

And then he died.

* * *

When all was silent, Mac came out from behind the door. He glanced at the scene. Later, he would remember it as being sort of like Romeo and Juliet but with bad guys instead of teenage lovers.

He went to the storage closet and let Lupe and Leslie out. Shielding them from the grisly slight, he hurried them away.

Allan Cole

CHAPTER THIRTY-FOUR

THE COAST GUARD chopper was once again heading for the speeding hovercraft, but this time it was backed up by two gunboats bounding over the waves toward the ship. A loudspeaker crackled.

"Unidentified hovercraft! This is the US Coast Guard! I repeat: US Coast Guard to unidentified hovercraft!"

Behind the bridge superstructure, Novarro was stacking boxes of explosives next to a large fuel storage tank. As he crimped the last wires into place, the chopper's lights moved across him.

Once again, the pilot's voice lashed out into the night: "Hovercraft. Heave to immediately, or we will open fire!"

Novarro laughed, grabbed the detonator box and ran back onto the bridge.

*   *   *

A moment later, Mac emerged from behind one of the Zodiacs. He started toward the boxes of explosives, but a gunman suddenly loomed out of the darkness. The guy grinned hugely.

"Well, lookit what we got here," he said. "Twenty thousand bucks on the friggin' hoof."

He practically had Mac dead right then and there, but as he raised his weapon to fire there was a loud "thump!" behind him. He whirled to see a young ship's officer stumbling out of the darkness, blood-spattered and looking like a zombie. And like a zombie he moaned "Nooooooo!" as he hurled himself at the gunman, who fired point blank.

Mac leaped for the gunman, clubbing him to the deck then snapping his neck in one smooth motion. He went to the man who lay breathing his last. He knelt over the young lieutenant.

"May God forgive me," the kid said.

Then he shuddered and died. Mac looked down at him then reached out and closed his staring eyes.

"I'm sure he will, pal," he said.

*   *   *

Mirasol was at the wheel, pinching out all the speed he could. He looked over as Novarro went to the com center and lifted the microphone.

Novarro glared out the window at the helicopter, which hovered only a few yards off the boat, and keyed the mike.

"Unidentified hovercraft to the US Coast Guard. This is your first and only warning."

*   *   *

Lt. Snow and Albert stared in shock as Novarro's voice boomed over the speaker.

"Stay away from this ship," he announced, "or I will blow it—and everyone aboard—to hell. Don't make the mistake of thinking that I'm bluffing. Fifty innocent lives are at stake."

"Christ," Snow said. "We don't have any God-damned choice. We have to back off."

The others nodded, resigned. Lt. Moon moved the steering stick, pulling the chopper to the side.

*   *   *

Novarro smiled as the lights of the helicopter and the gunboats retreated.

"We should probably get started," he said to Mirasol.

Mirasol nodded. He slowed the hovercraft down, letting it drop lower and lower in the water. When it came to a full stop, he rang the anchor room, and they heard the big chain rattling as the anchor splashed down. Then he picked up his command mike and keyed it.

*   *   *

Out on deck, a lone crewman moved through the deep shadows as Mirasol's voice boomed out.

"Lower the aft Zodiac."

"Si, Capitan," replied the crewman.

Allan Cole

He pulled a lever and a big lifting arm rose off the deck, the Zodiac gripped in its jaws. He pushed the boat toward the rail.

"Away the boat," Mirasol commanded.

"Si, Capitan."

He shoved the Zodiac past the rail until it hovered over the water. Then he signaled the bridge that everything was ready. There was a humming, and the cable rattled out, lowering it into the roiling seas.

Novarro exited the bridge, Mirasol just behind him. He advanced on the crewman, whose back was to him. He lifted his gun.

"Your arrogance finally got the better of you, MacGregor," he said.

The crewman hesitated then turned, his face gleaming under the deck lights.

Wearing gear stripped from a dead crewman, Mac looked at Novarro's gun then raised his hands. He was smiling.

"I can't believe you blew a perfectly good opportunity to shoot me in the back, Angel," he said. "That's your usual way, isn't it?"

Novarro shrugged. "Yes, of course, Every chance I get." Then he laughed. "This time, however, I have something different in mind." He leaned slightly to the side. "Ms. Martinez," he said, "I know you are in there watching. Come out, please. I don't intend to kill you...or your lover...just yet."

Lupe emerged from the inky shadows, Leslie at her side.

"So heartwarming," Novarro said. "Like a family reunited."

He motioned with the barrel of his gun, and Lupe and Leslie went to stand beside Mac.

"You'll be disgusted to know that the three of you will be aiding in my successful escape." He showed them the detonator. "There's a bomb on board, in case you haven't guessed," he said to Mac.

"I expected nothing less of you."

"I plan to blow it when we're well away." Novarro was enjoying himself.

"And the Coast Guard will be busy hunting victims instead of you," Mac said.

"Am I so transparent?"

"Like glass," Mac said.

Novarro chuckled. "Well, I'll allow you the last word, MacGregor. And reserve the last laugh for myself." He stretched out his hand. "But just in case you get the wrong idea…"

He grabbed Leslie. The girl shrieked. Mac moved to stop him, but a pistol butt across the forehead dropped him to his knees. Lupe leaped in, clawing. Mirasol grabbed her from behind and threw her to the deck.

"Let's go, Captain," Novarro said. "We've wasted enough time on my small pleasures."

Mirasol nodded and went over the rail. As he climbed down Novarro tucked a kicking Leslie under his arm and went after him.

"Uncle Mac! Uncle Mac!" she shouted.

Allan Cole

CHAPTER THIRTY-FIVE

LESLIE'S CRIES CUT through the haze of pain, and Mac forced himself to his knees. His head was streaming blood. He tried to get to his feet, but teetered, nearly falling over.

Lupe ran to him and helped him up. He stumbled to the rail, and they both looked down to see Mirasol pushing the Zodiac away with a pole. Novarro spotted them and grinned, keeping a firm grip on the struggling Leslie.

"The look on your face almost makes up for all the money you're costing me, MacGregor."

The mocking laughter had an unintended effect—jolting Mac into life. He vaulted over the rail and plummeted down on the Zodiac. He crashed against the rubber sides, bounced once then lunged out one hand.

Novarro thought Mac was reaching for him and staggered back, off-balance; his gun went off in the air.

But it was Leslie Mac was after, and as Mirasol rushed to his employer's aid, Mac snatched the child away and hurled himself backward into the water, carrying Leslie with him. Novarro recovered and opened fire just as they disappeared under the waves.

Under water, bullets plummeted harmlessly past them, leaving silver trails in the bright moonlight. Mac kept a firm grip on Leslie and kicked away from the Zodiac.

Then it was time to come up, and they rose to the surface. When their heads broke out of the water, he said, "Breathe, Leslie, breathe."

The girl sucked in air, then they both went under again just as Novarro opened fire. Mac struck deep, holding the girl in one arm, kicking for all he was worth. His injured head throbbed with pain and his ears rang.

He hoped to hell Leslie could hold on.

*   *   *

Navarro cursed as he emptied his weapon, ejected the clip and slammed in another. Marksman though he was, the tricky light of the moon fooled him and his shots went astray, splashing harmlessly in the water. He saw Mac surface briefly near the stern of the hovercraft. Obviously, he was trying to get the ship between him and his enemies.

"He's getting away," he shouted.

Mirasol only shook his head and returned to the Zodiac's controls.

"Forget him, Señor," he advised. "As you said, we have wasted enough time. Besides, the explosives should do the job for us."

Novarro saw his point. He nodded, and Mirasol zoomed away.

*   *   *

The moment they were gone Mac and Leslie edged back around the stern. He swam to the ladder and boosted the girl up. She started climbing to where Lupe waited, and he followed.

About halfway up, he stopped and turned to look out at the Zodiac. It had paused about fifty yards away. Novarro saw Mac looking at him and gave a cheerful wave. Then he aimed the detonator at him as if it were a gun.

He cupped his free hand around his mouth and shouted, "See you in Hell, MacGregor."

He toggled the switch and maybe—just maybe—there was a moment of realization and then the explosives hidden on the Zodiac erupted.

Mac watched the Zodiac become a huge ball of flame, then a column of thick, black smoke. He hung on the ladder a few moments, the flames reflected in his eyes.

"I don't hear you laughing, Novarro," he said.

Then he turned and climbed to where Lupe and Leslie waited.

Allan Cole

CHAPTER THIRTY-SIX

AT THE DOCKS, a Coast Guard cutter's ramp slammed down and fifty shouting, cheering kids poured off the ship toward a waiting bus. Nearby, an ambulance was parked, and a stoic Stormy sat in her wheelchair, anxiously looking at the faces of the happy children.

Leslie was not among them.

Then there was the whop, whop, whop of an approaching helicopter and Lt. Moon put his bird down on the tarmac. Stormy stared at it, trying not to hope.

Then Lupe climbed off, followed by Mac, who had Leslie in his arms. He saw Stormy and put Leslie down on the ground.

Stormy burst into tears, saying, damn, damn, damn, and Leslie ran toward her, arms spread wide, shouting, "Grandma. Grandma."

* * *

Mac held the small book with the picture of the coal-black horse on the cover. Lupe sat quietly beside him as he read to his unconscious daughter. He'd come every day for two weeks, reading Black Beauty to her. Now, he was nearing the end.

A nurse stood by the machines that kept Barbara technically alive. On the table next to her was a court order that permitted that situation to end.

In a fine, deep voice, Mac read:"'…My ladies have promised that I shall never be sold, and so I have nothing to fear; and here my story ends. My troubles are all over, and I am at home; and often before I am quite awake, I fancy I am still in the orchard at Birtwick, standing with my old friends under the apple-trees.'"

Mac finished, closed the book and looked at his daughter for a long, long time. Then he leaned down and kissed her, whispering:

"Good night, sweetheart."

THE END

Allan Cole

www.ingramcontent.com/pod-product-compliance
Lightning Source LLC
Chambersburg PA
CBHW071719140626
46557CB00012B/972